Frederic W. (Frederic William) MacDonald

Fletcher of Madeley

Frederic W. (Frederic William) MacDonald

Fletcher of Madeley

ISBN/EAN: 9783337003135

Printed in Europe, USA, Canada, Australia, Japan

Cover: Foto ©Andreas Hilbeck / pixelio.de

More available books at **www.hansebooks.com**

FLETCHER OF MADELEY.

BY THE REV.

FREDERIC W. MACDONALD,

*Theological Tutor, Handsworth College,
Birmingham.*

London:

HODDER AND STOUGHTON,

27, PATERNOSTER ROW.

MDCCCLXXXV.

PREFACE.

I HAVE to express my obligations to the Rev. L.
Tyerman for the help I have received in writing
this little book from his life of Fletcher, published
two years ago under the title of "Wesley's Designated
Successor." Mr. Tyerman's labours in the sphere of
Methodist history and biography are too well known
to require any word of commendation from me. It
may be enough to say that he has made it impossible
for any one to study the history of the great movement with which the names of Wesley, Whitefield, and
Fletcher are associated, without having recourse to his
volumes. There may be differences of opinion respecting Mr. Tyerman's judgments upon men and
things; there can be none whatever as to his patient,
laborious research, and perfect honesty in the use of
his ample materials.

I am also much indebted to my friends the Rev.
George Mather, now of Falmouth, and Mr. George
Stampe, of Great Grimsby, for the opportunity of exa-

mining a considerable number of Fletcher's manuscripts, hitherto unpublished. It was not to be
expected that fresh light could be thrown on Fletcher's
character, but these papers have enabled me to supply
some links, and add a few details to the story of his
life.

CONTENTS.

PAGE

CHAPTER I.

INTRODUCTORY 1

CHAPTER II.

EARLY LIFE 10

CHAPTER III.

SETTLES IN ENGLAND.—HIS CONNEXION WITH WESLEY
AND THE METHODISTS 19

CHAPTER IV.

SPIRITUAL DISCIPLINE 34

CHAPTER V.

ENTERS THE MINISTRY 44

CHAPTER VI.

FIRST YEARS AT MADELEY.—DIFFICULTIES AND DISCOUR-
AGEMENTS 56

CHAPTER VII.

CONTROVERSY AND CORRESPONDENCE 73

vii

CHAPTER VIII.

PAGE

TREVECCA COLLEGE.—THE CALVINIST CONTROVERSY . 95

CHAPTER IX.

WESLEY'S PROPOSAL.—FAILING HEALTH 119

CHAPTER X.

RESIDENCE IN SWITZERLAND 131

CHAPTER XI.

RETURN TO ENGLAND.—MARRIAGE 154

CHAPTER XII.

LAST YEARS. 168

APPENDIX 193

CHAPTER I.

INTRODUCTORY.

THERE is reason to think that the interest felt in the Evangelical Revival of the last century, after declining for awhile, is again steadily increasing. It may be said that this quickened interest is but part of a larger intellectual movement, of a reaction, in which we have passed from undue disparagement of the eighteenth century to an exaggerated estimate of its importance and value. Nor is it likely, when eighteenth century forms of literature, philosophy, and social life are being studied with so much sympathy, that the most prominent event in its religious history would escape attention.

There is some truth in this, but it is not the whole account of the matter. The fact is, and we are continually being reminded of it, the consequences of the Revival are by no means exhausted. We are not yet at the end of its manifestations; and though some of its later forms have new and striking features of their own, their relation to the original movement is attested both by historic descent and by inward resemblances and affinities. So long as this is the case, and the Revival, or Reformation, of a century and a half ago is still amongst the living forces that influence society, the interest with

B

which its rise and progress are regarded will continue. Active Christian spirits will seek to understand and respond to its newer developments; and
others, whether in sympathy with those developments
or not, will be obliged to take account of them, and
assign them, as far as possible, to their true succession
and order.

In addition to its direct, historical consequences,
moreover, time is continually discovering or suggesting
remoter and more complicated results of the Evangelical
Revival, thus rendering the study of the whole question
at once more difficult and more attractive. What were
its real relations, if any, to the teaching of Coleridge,
the points of agreement and divergence, of attraction
and repulsion between it and that original and influential
mind, to which so many, who in their turn have influenced the course of religious thought in - England,
have confessed themselves supremely indebted? What
is the connexion, revealed both by resemblances and
by contrasts, between the Evangelical Revival of the
eighteenth century and the Tractarian or Anglo-Catholic
movement of the nineteenth, between the Oxford of
John and Charles Wesley and the Oxford of Keble
and Pusey and Newman? What has the Revival con-
tributed to the gradual but unmistakable change that
has come over the theology of the Calvinistic Churches;
and, again, to the progress of democracy in Church
and State? As regards some at least of these questions,
it is too soon to look for precise and final answers;
but their relevance will be admitted, and the evidence

by which they must be determined accumulates from year to year.

While the interest in the Evangelical movement is thus reinforced from various quarters, time, in the exercise of its kindliest office, has removed a principal hindrance to a fair appreciation of it. Justice is now generally done to the character of its leaders, and the existing differences of opinion as to the value of their work are, for the most part, differences of which there is no need to be ashamed. It is no longer necessary to vindicate their memory from ignoble charges of fanaticism, hypocrisy, or ambition. To slander Wesley, or to ridicule Whitefield, has ceased to bring profit or to give pleasure to any one. Hardly a month passes but a monument is erected, a eulogy pronounced, a tribute paid to one or other of the men who, a hundred and fifty years ago, brought new life to the English Church and nation. Their reputation is not now a charge upon the loyalty of particular bodies of Christians, at once doing battle for themselves and for the character of their fathers and founders; they belong to the Churches, which are many, to the Church, which is One, and their names are in the keeping of the general company of Christians far and near.

And this change from the strife and bitterness of former days has come about, as such changes are wont to come, not so much by valiant advocacy or successful disputation, as by the sure working of God upon the hearts of men, enabling them to " discern between the righteous and the wicked, between him that serveth

God and him that serveth Him not." Sooner or later
this discernment comes, stealing through a thousand
channels of conviction into the heart and conscience
of a people, no one knows precisely when or how; and
far more weighty than any formal acts of canonization
are the verdicts by which the conscience of after ages
names its benefactors and heroes, often to the reversal
of the passionate judgments of earlier times. The monument of the Wesleys is in Westminster Abbey; Whitefield's
grave is in America; Fletcher's ashes lie in Madeley
churchyard. Each has his record in a fitting inscription; but their common epitaph, as men once persecuted for righteousness' sake, but now to be had in
everlasting remembrance, was written long before: "This
was he whom we had sometimes in derision, and a
proverb of reproach; we fools accounted his life madness, and his end to be without honour: how is he to
be numbered among the children of God, and his lot
is among the saints! . . . The righteous live for
evermore; their reward also is with the Lord, and the
care of them is with the Most High."

In the minutes of the Methodist Conference which
met at Bristol, in July, 1786, the following entry
occurs:

"*Q.* Who has died this year?

"*A.* John Fletcher, a pattern of all holiness, scarce
to be paralleled in a century."

Such is the brief record that marks the passing away

of a man whose place in the love and veneration of Wesley and of the Methodists was unique. Second only to the great leader himself in his influence, and in the special character of that influence leaving even Wesley behind, Fletcher's loss was the greatest sustained by the Revival from the death of Whitefield, in 1770, to that of Wesley, in 1791. One word in the short obituary notice reveals the secret of his power; it was *holiness.*

The term saint, in the New Testament extended to all the members of Christ, is often used colloquially to describe any one who, in comparison with worldly men or mere formal Christians, is conspicuous for reality and earnestness of spiritual life; but it may be applied to Fletcher in that last and highest sense, which makes it so rare a designation even of the best men. He possessed in an exceptional degree the qualities that constitute saintliness: deep humility and transparent purity, absolute unworldliness, with love unfailing, and patience that had its perfect work. The impression that he made upon those with whom he came in contact has been renewed upon biographers and historians.

"Fletcher was a saint," is the testimony of earlier and later witnesses. To none of his associates in the great Revival, the goodliest company of Christian men the age possessed, is this testimony borne in the same sense and with the same entire agreement. He was excelled by them in one respect and another; he could not, for example, sustain comparison for a moment with Wesley in the commanding powers, intellectual and moral, that

have placed him among the greatest leaders of the
Church Catholic; but for seraphic piety, for sanctity
that had no perceptible spot or flaw, Fletcher of Madeley
stood alone.   This is the deliberate judgment of those
who knew him best.   Of these Wesley was the chief.
In the funeral sermon which he preached soon after
Fletcher's death he said: "I was intimately acquainted
with him for above thirty years.   I conversed with him
morning, noon, and night, without the least reserve,
during a journey of many hundred miles.   And in all
that time I never heard him speak an improper word,
or saw him do an improper action.   To conclude:
Many exemplary men have I known, holy in heart and
life, within fourscore years; but one equal to him I have
not known, one so inwardly and outwardly devoted
to God.   So unblamable a character in every respect
I have not found either in Europe or America, and I
scarce expect to find another such on this side eternity."

Benson, for many years the intimate friend of Fletcher,
wrote to Wesley as follows: "I have often thought
the testimony that Bishop Burnet bears of Archbishop
Leighton might be borne of him with equal propriety:
'After an intimate acquaintance of many years, and
after being with him by night and by day, at home
and abroad, in public and in private, . . . I must
say, I never heard an idle word drop from his lips, or
any conversation which was not to the use of edifying.
I never saw him in any temper in which I myself would
not have wished to be found at death.'   Any one who

has been intimately acquainted with Mr. Fletcher will say the same of him, and they who knew him best will say it with the most assurance."

All other contemporary notices of Fletcher are in the same strain. So with the historians and biographers of subsequent times. "Fletcher in any communion would have been a saint," says Southey. "He was a saint," wrote Isaac Taylor, "as unearthly a being as could tread the earth at all." "Fletcher," says Robert Hall, "is a seraph who burns with the ardour of Divine love. Spurning the fetters of mortality, he almost habitually seems to have anticipated the rapture of the beatific vision."

These testimonies may be closed, though they are not exhausted, by a passage from one of the most recent and valuable works on the religious life of the last century:[1] "If John Wesley was the great leader and organiser, Charles Wesley the great poet, and George Whitefield the great preacher of Methodism, the highest type of saintliness which it produced was unquestionably John Fletcher. Never perhaps since the rise of Christianity has the mind which was in Christ Jesus been more faithfully copied than it was in the Vicar of Madeley. To say that he was a good Christian is saying too little. He was more than Christian, he was Christlike."

Fletcher's first biographer was John Wesley. In the

---

[1] "The English Church in the Eighteenth Century." By C. J. Abbey and J. H. Overton. Vol. ii., p. 113.

preface to the funeral sermon preached in London on
November 6th, 1785, he says: "I hastily put together
some memorials of ·this great man, intending, if God
permit, when I have more leisure and more materials,
to write a fuller account of his life." Twelve months
later, being then in the eighty-fourth year of his age, the
following entry appears in his "Journal": "*Oct. 25th,
1786.* I now applied myself in earnest to the writing
of Mr. Fletcher's life, having procured the best materials
I could. To this I dedicated all the time I could
spare till November, from five in the morning till
eight at night. These are my studying hours; I cannot
write longer in a day without hurting my eyes." The
labour of love was soon completed, and Wesley published "A Short Account of the Life and Death of the
Rev. John Fletcher," with the motto, "Sequor, non
passibus æquis." That was no conventional eulogy—
Wesley did not deal in them,—but, as we have seen, his
heart's tribute to the holiest man he had ever known.
And if the venerable Wesley counted himself but as one
who followed, and that at a distance, the saintly Vicar
of Madeley, he would be a hardy writer who could set
himself to portray such a life and character unvisited
by misgivings and unchastened by the responsibility that
comes from the study of high examples of Christian
holiness. But for the reader also, if his heart is as the
writer's, there will be a share alike in the humiliation
and in the hopes which the study of a holy life may well
afford. This brief memoir of Fletcher of Madeley is
attempted because no lapse of time or change of cir-

cumstances can make it unseasonable to contemplate a character like his.   Such men do not die :

> "——a sweet and virtuous soul,
> Like seasoned timber, never gives ;
> But though the whole world turn to coal,
> Then chiefly lives."

CHAPTER II.

EARLY LIFE.

(1729–1750.)

JOHN FLETCHER was a Swiss by birth and education. His name was properly Jean Guillaume de
la Fléchère. The origin of the anglicized form that he
afterwards adopted is thus explained by himself: "Soon
after I came to England my English friends, complaining
of the length of my Swiss name, began to contract it by
dropping the French syllables of it. So they called me
Fletcher, and by that name I have been known among
the English ever since." He came of an old and respectable family, not without distinguished connexions.
His father had, in early life, held a commission in the
French army, but, retiring from the service in order to
marry, had returned to his native country, where he
became a colonel in the militia, and *Assesseur Baillival*,
or assistant judge, of Nyon. Here he resided in a fine
old house in the outskirts of the town, not rich, but
possessing a modest fortune and considerable local influence; and here John Fletcher, the youngest of eight
children, was born on September 12th, 1729.

Nyon is an old town dating from Roman times. It is
about fifteen miles from Geneva, on the northern shore

of the lake, picturesquely placed at the water's edge, with
the Jura Mountains rising in the distance behind, and
the mountains of Savoy magnificently visible across the
lake in front. The passion for Swiss scenery had not
then become common and conventional. Some fifty
years later Gibbon mentions it as of recent origin,
counting it "a misfortune rather than a merit that the
situation and beauty of the Pays de Vaud . . . and
the fashion of viewing the mountains and glaciers have
opened us on all sides to the incursions of foreigners."
Fletcher was not before his time with regard to this most
modern of sentiments or susceptibilities. There is little
trace of impressions made on him either by the grandeur
or the loveliness of his native scenery. In a letter written when, at fifty years of age, he was revisiting Nyon, he
invites a friend to come to "this delightful country, and
share a pleasant apartment, and one of the finest prospects in the world in the house where I was born. . . .
We have a fine, shady wood near the lake, where I can
ride in the cool all the day, and enjoy the singing of
a multitude of birds." And then he adds, "But this,
though sweet, does not come up to the singing of my
dear friends in England."

Fletcher received his early education at a school in
Nyon, and was then sent, with his two brothers, to the
Academy, now the University, of Geneva, where he
spent seven years in diligent and successful study. On
leaving Geneva he spent some time at Lenzburg, chiefly
for the sake of learning German. In the scanty
records of his youth there is a remarkable succession of

perils and hairbreadth escapes.   Fletcher was a bold
and skilful swimmer, and on at least two occasions his
adventurousness nearly cost him his life.   Once he swam
with a companion to a small, rocky island, about five
miles from the shore of the lake.   They found it so
steep and smooth that they could not land, and it was
not until they were completely exhausted by swimming
round it that they came upon a place where they could
crawl ashore, and whence they were rescued by a passing boat.   The other adventure was still more perilous.
He was swimming in the Rhine, and was drawn unawares
into the mid-stream, where, he says, "the water was
extremely rough, and poured along like a galloping
horse."   After a long and desperate struggle with the
current, he was carried into a mill-race, and hurled
among the piles on which the mill stood.   A blow on
the breast made him senseless, and he knew nothing
more till he rose on the other side of the mill, after
being among the piles for twenty minutes, to find himself five miles from the place where he had started.
Another time, when he and his brother were fencing with
swords blunted with a kind of button fixed upon the
point, the button on his brother's weapon broke, and
Fletcher received a desperate thrust in the side that had
well-nigh killed him.   These incidents have often been
referred to as illustrations of the Providence that directed
his life; but they reveal in addition elements of character that should not be overlooked.   There was nothing
effeminate in him.   On this point a mistake may be
made.   It is possible to misinterpret the delicate fea-

tures, with thei rapt expression, the almost excessive modesty, the language fuller charged with emotion than is quite our English wont. But there was strength, not weakness, beneath these often misread indications of character. The natural man in John Fletcher was a soldier and an athlete, and these qualities of manhood remained with him to the end, though turned to higher issues and manifest in other forms than in these early years.

From childhood Fletcher had a tender conscience and a devout spirit, and was exceptionally free from fault. He says, " I think it was when I was seven years of age that I first began to feel the love of God shed abroad in my heart, and that I resolved to give myself up to Him, and to the service of His Church, if ever I should be fit for it." Years afterwards there came for him a time of spiritual conflict, of heart-searching, and deep repentance, from which he passed into the clear light of reconciliation with God through faith in Christ; but his conversion had this in common with Wesley's, that it crowned and completed the piety of his youth. In both cases conversion was a momentous, unmistakable epoch; but not by reason of any change from reckless and ungodly living. It was one of those supreme events in the history of the soul that has its foundations and beginnings long before. Its relation to the past is not, outwardly at least, one of contrast, and inwardly it is not wholly so. The continuity of the spiritual life is not broken, but rather a stage is reached where the discipline and endeavours of previous years, having served their

end, pass into a larger liberty and a more abundant life.
" It pleased God to reveal His Son in me," is the true
account, not only of sudden conversions, properly so
called, but of that last act of grace which brings devout
and serious youth to the full knowledge of Him whom
they have long sought, and served while yet seeking.

Fletcher's student life seems to have been wholly free
from the vices which, both then and now, are too generally counted venial, or even natural and reasonable, in
youth.   His subsequent self-upbraidings were deep
enough, but they must not be misunderstood.   When
he says, in a letter written to his brother in his 26th
year, " My infancy was vicious, and my youth still more
so," the reference is not to open, actual sins, but to that
ignorance of the true Christian life which, apprehended
in its full significance, appears to the regenerate conscience as the one root-evil.   His confessions have little
.in common with those of Augustine, or Bunyan, or John
Newton.   The most particular allusion they contain is
the following : " I formed an acquaintance with some
deists, at first with the design of converting them, and
afterwards with the pretence of thoroughly examining
their sentiments.   But my heart, like that of Balaam,
was not right with God.   He abandoned me, and I
enrolled myself in their party.   A considerable change
took place in my deportment.   Before, I had a form of
religion, and now I lost it; but as to the state of my
heart, it was precisely the same.   I did not remain many
weeks in this state ; the Good Shepherd sought after
me, a wandering sheep.   Again I became professedly a

Christian; that is, I resumed a regular attendance at church and the communion, and offered up frequent prayers in the name of Jesus Christ. There were also in my heart some sparks of true love to God, and some germs of genuine faith; but a connexion with worldly characters, and an undue anxiety to promote my secular interests, prevented the growth of these Christian graces."

It had been Fletcher's desire as a child to become a Christian minister. This object was still kept in view during his studies at Geneva, and appears to have been approved by his family; but as he entered his twentieth year his views underwent a considerable change, the notion of entering the ministry was abandoned, and he sought a military career instead. One or two reasons may be assigned for this change. He feared he was unfit for the ministry. Though outwardly of blameless life, he felt, as the time for ordination drew near, his need of true faith in Christ and love to God, and shrank from an office for which these were the first requisites. Further, a doctrinal difficulty disclosed itself. " I was disgusted by the necessity I should be under to subscribe the doctrine of predestination"; and while thus religiously and doctrinally disturbed, the influence of certain friends combined with his own inclination to suggest that frequent resource of the more adventurous youth of Switzerland, military service in some foreign army. Fletcher's father had served the king of France, why should not he take service under the king of Portugal, who was about to send troops to Brazil? Accordingly, disregarding his father's remonstrances, but following his

example, he made his way to Lisbon, raised a company
of his countrymen, doubtless by the method embodied
in the proverb, " Pas d'argent, pas de Suisse," and received a captain's commission in the Portuguese service.
This kind of professional soldiership, for which no patrio-
tism or devotion to a noble cause could be pleaded,
did not shock the general conscience in Fletcher's day.
It presented no difficulty to his own. That such a
vocation is in our own day generally condemned, being
barely tolerated under the most extenuating circumstances, is an illustration of progress in morals and religion,—one of many that may be set over against
some discouraging aspects of the times.

Meanwhile Fletcher is waiting in Lisbon for a re-
mittance from home which does not arrive. His parents
disapprove of this Portuguese-Brazilian venture, and refuse to send him money. But his mind is made up, and
with or without money he will go. An unlooked for
hindrance, however, prevents. A servant waiting upon
him at breakfast let fall a kettle of hot water, and so
scalded his leg as to lay him helpless in bed. In the
meantime the ship sailed for Brazil without him, and
was never heard of again.

On his recovery he returned to Switzerland, there
being no further prospect of employment in the Portuguese service. But his desire for military life was
unabated. His uncle and eldest brother were in the
Dutch service, and in a little while he received word
that his uncle had procured a commission for him. He
at once set out for Flanders, but before he could join

the army the Peace of Aix-la-Chapelle, in October, 1748, entirely altered the situation. Troops were disbanded or sent home, and the uncle on whom his hopes depended left the service, and died soon afterwards. With his death Fletcher's hopes were entirely destroyed, and he abandoned all thoughts of becoming a soldier.

The first well-marked stage of his history was now completed. He had reached manhood. He had received the best education that his age and his country afforded. In temperament he was active and ardent, in spirit serious and devout; and though he had declined from his early piety, he was entirely free from the follies and vices so easily learnt, and so readily condoned, at college and in camp. It was impossible to say how a life with such preparations would open out. That its promise was fair, and even noble, might well be judged; but that it should find at once the supply of its own deepest want, and the sphere for the employment of its powers, in a foreign country, and in connexion with a religious movement wholly unknown in Switzerland, and unsanctioned either by Church or society in England, was among the things that could not possibly be foreseen. Lives like Fletcher's, when they lie complete before us, are luminous in the linked succession of divinely directed steps; the overruling Providence is so manifest that nothing which takes place surprises us; but, followed in their natural order, the determining events are unforeseen, they come in unlikely forms and from quarters whence they could not be expected. From Swiss Moderatism Fletcher was

C

to pass into the bosom of English Methodism. The
student reared in the school of Calvin and Beza was
to be the apologist of Evangelical Arminianism. He
was to become, not

> " Captain, or colonel, or knight-in-arms "

in Portugal, Brazil, or Flanders, but " Vicar of Madeley."
But of all this he knew nothing ;—how could he ?

> " I know that the way of man is not in himself :
> It is not in man that walketh to direct his steps."

———

> "Keep Thou my feet ; I do not ask to see
> The distant scene ; one step enough for me."

CHAPTER III.

BEING now without occupation, or any definite prospect of it, Fletcher determined to visit England. It does not appear that he had any motive for doing so beyond a desire to travel and to acquire the English language. Accordingly, some time in 1749 or 1750—it is impossible to fix the date more precisely—he came to London, well supplied apparently with money, but with the slenderest stock of English. At the custom house he and his companions seem to have been somewhat roughly treated, and their letters of introduction were taken from them on the ground that all letters must be sent by the post. His first adventure in London bade fair to be of the sort that London has often provided for newly arrived and trustful youth. He handed over his purse, containing some £90, to a stranger, a Jew, who offered to get his money changed for him. To the honour of this unknown Jew, let it be recorded that Fletcher's simplicity was not abused. He returned in due time, and brought the full amount in English coin.

The first eighteen months of his residence in England Fletcher spent in the house of a Mr. Burchell, who kept a school near Hatfield. Here he acquired a good knowledge of English, beside continuing his general studies. On leaving Mr. Burchell, in the year 1752, he received the appointment of tutor to the two sons of Mr. Thomas Hill, of Tern Hall, in Shropshire. This position he retained for nearly seven years, dividing his time between Shropshire and London, according as Mr. Hill's family accompanied him to town for the sitting of Parliament, or remained in the country.

Through all this time there is no sign of any wish on Fletcher's part to return to Switzerland; and it is at first sight a little perplexing that his visit to England should have developed into something very like a permanent residence, when as yet he had no definite calling, and the powerful influences of a great spiritual change had not come into existence. But there is a reasonable explanation to be found in the state of things in his native country, where a gentleman's younger son, disinclined for the ministry and disappointed of a commission in the army, had no great choice of a career. On this matter we have the testimony of an exceptionally keen and competent observer. The early years of Fletcher's residence in England correspond very closely with those of Gibbon's first period of residence in Switzerland. From 1753 to 1758, years spent by Fletcher in the family of Mr. Hill, the youthful Gibbon was living under the roof of M. Pavilliard, a Calvinist minister at Lausanne. It was about the close of this period that he wrote, for the benefit of a Swiss friend, a short paper upon political and social life in Switzerland, an essay that is doubly worth reading, for its own sake, and as exhibiting the powers and the promise in early manhood of the future historian. An extract or two will show some aspects of the society that Fletcher had so lately left, and to which he never really returned, and will suggest the explanation of that readiness to "forget his own people and his father's house," which has perplexed some of his critics and biographers :

"Even to the present day, a secret inquisition still reigns at Lausanne, where the names of Arminian and Socinian are often mentioned in the letters written by very honest people to their patrons of Berne ; and offices are often given or withheld according to the reports made of the religious tenets of the candidates. . . . In aristocratical republics the citizens of one town are not contented with being sovereigns collectively, unless they individually appropriate all offices of honour or emolument. In the canton of Berne talents and information are not of the smallest use to any one who is not born in the capital ; and in another sense they are useless to those born there, because they *must* make their way without them. Their subjects in the Pays de Vaud are condemned, by the circumstances of their birth, to a condition of shameful obscurity. They naturally become therefore a prey to despair, and neglecting to cultivate talents which they can never enjoy an opportunity to display, those who had capacities for becoming great men are contented

with making themselves agreeable companions.   Should
I propose that the subjects obtained a right to hold the
lucrative employments of *baillis*, or governors of dis-
tricts, the aristocratical families of Berne would think
me guilty of a crime little less than sacrilege.   'The
emoluments of these offices form the patrimony of the
State ; and we are the State.'   It is true that you in
the Pays de Vaud may be deputies to the *baillis ;* but
the advantages belonging to that subordinate magistracy
are obtained on certain conditions, which, unless the
holder of the office lives a certain number of years,
renders his bargain a very bad one for his family.

"What encouragement is then left for the gentlemen
of the Pays de Vaud ?   That of foreign service.   But
to them even this road to preferment is extremely
difficult, and to attain the higher ranks is impossible. ·
.   .   .   In his own district every *bailli* is at the
head of religion, of the law, the army, and the finances.
As judge, he decides without appeal all causes to the
amount of a hundred francs—a sum of little importance
to a gentleman, but which often makes the whole
fortune of a peasant ; and he decides alone, for the
voices of his assessors have not any weight in the scale.
He confers, or rather he sells, all the employments in
his district."

It is unnecessary further to multiply extracts from this
letter.   The relevancy to Fletcher's personal history of
those just cited will be obvious.   He belonged, not
to the aristocracy of Berne, but to the subordinate
gentry of the Pays de Vaud.   The office held by his

father was not that of *bailli*, with its great emoluments
and privileges, but the very inferior office of *assesseur*.
Fletcher was one of those to whom little remained but
foreign service, and we have seen how eagerly he sought
it, and by what circumstances his hopes were frustrated.
And so it was, we take it, that, having come to England,
he scarcely knew why, the quiet life of a scholar and
tutor satisfied him till such time as, in the possession
of a new religious life and an absorbing vocation, he
found " foreign service " in the highest and holiest
warfare. It was while living in Mr. Hill's family
that Fletcher came under the influences which determined his whole future course. He now first became
acquainted with the Methodists.

Some fifteen years had elapsed since Wesley formed
the first Methodist society, and Whitefield, shut out
from the churches, had begun to preach the gospel to
the wondering crowds on Kingswood Hill and Ken-
nington Common. Wesley's own ungarnished account
fixes the exact date of one of the most significant
events in modern Church history. It is as follows : " In
the latter end of the year 1739 eight or ten persons
came to me in London, who appeared to be deeply
convinced of sin, and earnestly groaning for redemption.
They desired I would spend some time with them in
prayer, and advise them how to flee from the wrath to
come. That we might have more time for this great
work, I appointed a day when they might all come
together, which from thenceforward they did every
Thursday in the evening. To these, and as many

more as desired to join with them (for the number increased daily), I gave those advices from time to time which I judged most needful for them; and we always concluded our meeting with prayer suited to their several necessities. This was the rise of the United Society, first in London, and then in other places."

It was not however to the members of this society that the name of Methodist was first applied, still less was it a designation adopted by the society itself. It originated, some years earlier, in Oxford, as a nickname for the Wesleys and a few other university men, who used to meet together to read the Scriptures, and endeavoured generally to order their lives with a religious precision rare enough in the Oxford of those days. To quote Wesley's words again : " The exact regularity of their lives, as well as studies, -occasioned a young gentleman of Christ Church to say, ' Here is a new set of Methodists sprung up,' alluding to some ancient physicians who were so called. The name was new and quaint, so it took immediately, and the Methodists were known all over the university."

But this first, or Oxford, Methodism was now a thing of the past. The Methodism that Fletcher found in England was really another and very different thing, though called by the same name. It was separated from the former, not only by a score or so of years, but by spiritual changes and developments of the most important character. The first Methodists were, above all things, students and Churchmen. They revived the observance of long neglected canons and rubrics; they moulded their lives on ascetic models, fasting on Wednesdays and Fridays, and eating no flesh during Lent except on Saturdays and Sundays. They thought and spoke much of Christian antiquity, and, like the Oxford leaders of a century later, sought in that venerable past a rule and an authority co-ordinate with Scripture. They read Thomas à Kempis and Bishop Taylor and the great High Church mystic of their own day, William Law. This Oxford Methodism, with its almost monastic rigours, its living by rule, its canonical hours of prayer, is a fair and noble phase of the many-sided life of the Church of England, and, with all its defects and limitations, claims our deep respect. But it was not the instrument by which the Church and nation were to be revived; it had no message for the world, no secret of power with which to move and quicken the masses. To do this it must become other than it was. It must die, in order to bring forth much fruit. And this death and rising again were accomplished in the spiritual change wrought in John Wesley, the leader of the earlier and of the later Methodism. What was that change?

In the year 1738, on his return from Georgia, Wesley writes: "It is now two years and almost four months since I left my native country, in order to teach the Georgian Indians the nature of Christianity. But what have I learned myself meantime? Why, what I the least of all suspected: that I, who went to America to convert others, was never myself converted to God."

Now it may be urged, with some show of reason, as indeed his own language in later life implies, that Wesley was not, in the full sense of the term, an unconverted man during the whole of his Oxford life and of his residence in Georgia. But nothing is more certain than the reality and importance of the change through which he now passed. His apprehension of salvation by faith in Christ had been hitherto obscure and imperfect. He found no rest for his soul. He longed to be at peace with God. "The faith which I want is a sure trust and confidence in God that, through the merits of Christ, my sins are forgiven, and I reconciled to the favour of God, . . . that faith which enables every one that hath it to cry out, 'I live not, but Christ liveth in me; and the life which I now live, I live by faith in the Son of God, who loved me, and gave Himself for me.'" It is not necessary to repeat here the oft-told story of Wesley's acquaintance with the Moravians, and more particularly with Peter Böhler, by whose teaching and testimony he was convinced that the one thing wanting to him was a living faith in Christ, together with that assurance of forgiveness and power over sin that are its fruits. How much had to be surrendered before a man of Wesley's training and attainments could submit himself to the conception of saving faith that was now presented to him, may be learnt from his own statements. It is enough to say that he found that way of faith in Christ which is the open secret of the gospel, at once "hidden from the wise and prudent, and revealed unto

babes." He received the reconciliation and rejoiced
in God. "I felt I did trust in Christ, Christ alone,
for salvation; and an assurance was given me that He
had taken away my sins, even mine, and saved me
from the law of sin and death." This was Wesley's
"conversion." Whether rightly so called or not, there
is no doubt as to the change itself, and its results.
Henceforth he was a new man, ready for a new work.
Instead of directing the religious life of a handful of
devout university men, he traversed the land in every
direction, preaching to the multitudes and organizing
societies for Christian fellowship. Religion was no
longer a painful quest, a high endeavour, a discipline,
but a life bright with the Divine favour and filled with
unspeakable blessings, offered to all men through faith
in Christ. Peace with God, the witness and fruit of
the Spirit, the blessings of sonship and sanctification,—
these were not the rewards of fidelity and endurance,
the privilege of the few; they were included in the
common salvation. Every sinner might seek them,
every believer would find them. There is no mistaking
the difference between this gospel, soon to be preached in
every town and village of England, and the teaching that
nourished the austere piety of the Oxford Methodists.
As an able writer has put it, "The birthday of a Christian was shifted from his baptism to his conversion,
and in that change the partition line of two great
systems is crossed." Some will reckon this change a
grave error, and all that came of it to be but a falling
away from a high beginning. They will find in the

ascetic, churchly pietists of the earlier time their true
Wesley and their ideal Methodism; but time and history
have borne a testimony from which there is, practically,
no appeal.   The Methodism that revived the Church
and awakened the nation was not that of the "Holy
Club" at Oxford.   It differed from it as Wesley after
"conversion" differed from his former self.   Its spirit,
its methods, its watchwords were altered.   Something
may have been lost when Methodism moved from its
academic birthplace into the work-day world, but more
was gained.   It had found what it had long sought.
It knew now what salvation meant.   "I waited patiently
for the Lord; and He inclined unto me, and heard my
cry. He   .   .   .   set my feet upon a rock, and established my goings.   And He hath put a new song in
my mouth, even praise unto our God : many shall see it,
and fear, and shall trust in the Lord."

By the time that Fletcher became acquainted with
Methodism it had passed through some important stages
of its history.   It had reached its highest point in the
favour of a small section of the aristocracy, and had
encountered its strongest opposition among the people.
Never in subsequent years were so many persons of
rank associated with Methodism as in its first two or
three decades; and never in later times have its followers endured afflictions like those which the first
Methodists suffered in Staffordshire, in Yorkshire, and
in Cornwall.   It had now secured something like peace
for its persecuted people; its travelling preachers crossed
and recrossed the entire country; its societies contained

many thousands of members, won for the most part from ignorance and irreligion; and with restless yet disciplined activity it was appreciably influencing the national life. Religion, which had seemed to "stand on tiptoe in our land," turned again to its ancient seats, and to the home it had well-nigh forsaken. There was hope for Christianity among us yet.

It was during one of Fletcher's journeys to London with Mr. Hill's family that he first met with the people called Methodists. The story is told by Wesley: "While they stopped at St. Albans, he walked out into the town, and did not return till they were set out for London. A horse being left for him, he rode after, and overtook them in the evening. Mr. Hill asked him why he stayed behind. He said, 'As I was walking I met with a poor old woman, who talked so sweetly of Jesus Christ, that I knew not how the time passed away.' 'I shall wonder,' said Mrs. Hill, 'if our tutor does not turn Methodist by-and-by.' 'Methodist, madam,' said he; 'pray, what is that?' She replied, 'Why, the Methodists are a people that do nothing but pray; they are praying all day and all night.' 'Are they?' said he; 'then, by the help of God, I will find them out, if they be above ground.' He did find them out not long after, and was admitted into the society."

Amongst the Methodists Fletcher learnt what Wesley had learnt from the Moravians, that there was something in religion to which he was yet a stranger. Like so many others of fine moral nature and virtuous habits, he was much perplexed as to the nature of saving faith.

"Is it possible," he writes, "that I, who have always been accounted so religious, who have made divinity my study, and received the Premiums of Piety (so called) from the university for my writings on Divine subjects,—is it possible that I should yet be so ignorant as not to know what faith is?" He came to the conclusion that this was so. His past life, so free from outward sin, appeared to him to be sinful beyond expression. It had no foundation in Christ. He had lived to himself. His righteousness was self-righteousness, it was as filthy rags. He now heard sermons, but was only the more convinced that he was an unbeliever; he wrote out a confession of his sins, misery, and helplessness, but had no heart to finish it. He feared he did not even yet mourn enough for his sins; "but I found relief in Mr. Wesley's "Journal," where I learned that we should not build on what we feel, but that we should go to Christ with all our sins and hardness of heart." Deliverance however was at hand. The salvation that he longed for drew near. He trusted in Christ, and found rest to his soul. His bonds were broken. He was filled with joy and peace through believing. Henceforth, "the life that he lived in the flesh, he lived by the faith of the Son of God."

It is surely worthy of remark that the chief leaders of the Evangelical Revival were converted in mature life, not after a wild and reckless, but after a more than commonly religious youth. Among the associates soon to be gathered around them a very different type of spiritual history may be discerned. Many of these had been notoriously sinful, and their conversion had all the dramatic completeness which belongs to a sudden transformation of conduct and character. But of the Wesleys and Whitefield at Oxford, and subsequently of Fletcher, it might be said that they were "touching the righteousness which is in the law, blameless." They fasted and prayed, and frequented the sacrament; they read religious books; they visited the sick and taught the ignorant; they eschewed all self-indulgence, were scrupulous in respect of duty, and consistently devout in spirit and manner. And yet the change wrought in them when they obtained a saving faith in Christ could not have been really greater if there had been a previous life of sin and folly to escape from. When a man passes from a righteousness of his own "which is of the law," to "that which is through faith in Christ," it is as truly a birth from above as when he is turned from sin to righteousness. The inner power and significance of conversion are the same in both cases. But this is widely misunderstood. That the wicked should be, if possible, converted, is generally held to be desirable. Society, even when most cynical and worldly, does, in a manner, hold that it behoves evil doers, especially among the lower orders, to repent of their sins and mend their ways; but that good people should call themselves sinners, that scholars and gentlemen of excellent character—whose only fault indeed was that of being righteous overmuch —should be anxious about their souls, and make other respectable people as uneasy as themselves, caused much irritation and perplexity.

It was, however, not the least of God's mercies to the Church and nation that the Revival began as it did with the conversion of good men, that its first witnesses and workers were not reclaimed profligates, but representatives of all that was best in the existing social order. If the gospel was to awaken the conviction of sin in such men as these, if it was to disclose to them deep spiritual needs, and set them asking what they must do to be saved, then society had misunderstood the whole matter, —which indeed was pretty nearly the case. Society's discernment of evil when it takes the form of crime is sufficiently acute ; concerning vice also it has convictions more or less emphatic: but of *sin, as sin,* its notions are feeble and confused. And that confusion and inadequacy of view are shared by the Church when men's need of Christ and His salvation is measured by the more or less of their outward good behaviour ; as though conversion were necessary for wicked and worthless members of the community, while those of a better sort can see the kingdom of God without being born from above. The history and experience of its leaders, humanly speaking, preserved the Revival from this error, and from the first guarded the doctrine of the new birth from one of its most common and practical perversions. The notion that while there are some people too bad to be converted there are others too good to require it, was doubly disproved. The early Methodist preachers moved joyously and confidently through the land, proclaiming a salvation which the worst might obtain, and which the best must not refuse or neglect.

From the time of his conversion to the close of his life Fletcher was a Methodist. The exact date when he joined the society cannot be determined, but in the year 1756 he was a member of a class in London, of which a Mr. Richard Edwards was the leader. His "class ticket," bearing the name "John Fletcher," and the date "Feb., 1757," lies before us as we write.

CHAPTER IV.

SPIRITUAL DISCIPLINE.

IT was in the beginning of the year 1755, when
Fletcher was in the twenty-sixth year of his age, that
he passed through the great change described in the last
chapter. For nearly five years he continued to live in
Mr. Hill's family, dividing his time, as before, between
Shropshire and London. Towards the close of that
period, however, new duties and engagements were opening out before him, and in 1760, when his pupils entered
the University of Cambridge, Fletcher's tutorship was at
an end.

His residence at Tern Hall was in many respects a
happy one for Fletcher. His duties were comparatively
light, and his situation was favourable to that life of
meditation, prayer, study, and self-discipline to which he
was so powerfully drawn. On Sundays he attended the
parish church of Atcham, a village near Shrewsbury.
When the service was over he usually walked home
alone by the Severn side. After a while these walks
were shared by a pious man named Vaughan, then in
Mr. Hill's service, who, in after years, gave the following account of them to Mr. Wesley :

"It was our ordinary custom, when the church ser-

vice was over, to retire into the most lonely fields or
meadows, where we frequently either kneeled down or
prostrated ourselves on the ground.   At those happy
seasons I was a witness of such pleadings and wres-
tlings with God, such exercises of faith and love, as I
have not known in any one ever since.   The consola-
tions which we then received from God induced us to
appoint two or three nights in a week, when we duly
met, after his pupils were asleep.   We met also constantly on Sunday between four and five in the morning.   Sometimes I stepped into his study on other days.
I rarely saw any book before him, besides the Bible and
the ' Christian Pattern.' "

Another, who knew him at that time, says that when
there was company to dinner at Mr. Hill's, Fletcher
would often get himself excused from being present,
and retire into the garden, to dine on a piece of bread
and a little fruit.   There are many testimonies to his
lifelong abstemiousness, but at this period it reached
a point of asceticism, concerning which Wesley has
recorded his judgment : " None can doubt if these austerities were well intended ; but it seems they were not
well judged.   It is probable they gave the first wound
to an excellent constitution, and laid the foundation of
many infirmities, which nothing but death could cure."
Again, referring to his manner of life at Madeley,
several years after, Wesley says : " He did not allow
himself such food as was necessary to sustain nature.
He seldom took any regular meals except he had company ; otherwise, twice or thrice in four-and-twenty hours

he ate some bread and cheese, or fruit. Instead of this he sometimes took a draught of milk, and then wrote on again."

That all this was unwise, and brought its own punishment, will be readily admitted; but it is well to note that Fletcher's ascetic practice was not the result of an ascetic theology. Beyond most holy men Fletcher apprehended and rejoiced in the freedom of the children of God. The last touch of the spirit of bondage disappeared at his conversion, and henceforth he was no more a servant but a son, walking in the clearest light, and possessing the strongest witness to his adoption. His rigid self-denial, his almost unearthly indifference to the common comforts and recreations of human life, his carefully ordered devotions, were not the travail of a soul going about to establish its own righteousness, nor the half-expiatory sacrifices of one who seeks to pacify his conscience or appease his restless longings. Beneath his ascetic practice was evangelical doctrine, and a living faith. He did not fast, and give whole days to study and whole nights to prayer, because he was in doubt or distress concerning his soul, but from his very joy in God, and delight in all that lifted him from things beneath to things above. His was the asceticism of ·love, and not of bondage or of fear.

By the help of manuscripts carefully preserved, though not hitherto made public, it is possible to draw very near to the devotional life of Fletcher at this period of his history. A document which affords pathetic insight into the depth and thoroughness of his consecration of himself to God now lies before us. It is a solemn covenant, drawn up in Latin, and covers the two sides of a parchment some nine inches by five in size. It is exquisitely written in a round, legible hand. The opening sentence, which is in Greek, reads thus : " In the name of God, the Creator of heaven and earth, Amen. O most high Jehovah, only God, Father, Son, and Holy Ghost, I, the vilest of the vile, worst of the sons of Adam, an apostate spirit, a man utterly undone, . . . resolve to consecrate myself to Thee, my Creator, Redeemer, Sanctifier." In the humblest strain of penitential confession, he proceeds to offer and present himself to God through the merits of Jesus Christ. The recurring phrase of consecration is, " Do, reddo, dico, dedico " (I give, restore, devote, dedicate); and all that he has, or is, or may be, is brought within this form of dedication. The formula of supplication is, " Peto, rogo, posco, flagito " (I ask, entreat, implore, importune); and in these terms he prays for pardon, grace, guidance, and final deliverance. There is reason to think that the signature, now almost illegible, was written with his own blood. After the manner of the earlier nonconformists, among whom the practice of drawing up solemn forms of covenant with God prevailed, Fletcher kept by him through life this sign and memorial of deliberate consecration to God, and renewed from time to time both its general vow and its detailed promises. It is dated August 24th, 1754.

Some two years later he prepared for his own use a

little manual of devotions, which is perhaps the most *vital* of all the Fletcher relics still preserved, as revealing more directly than any other his interior life, and the spirit and method of his daily devotions. It is a small, square book, strongly bound in leather, containing about two hundred closely written pages.

More than half of its contents are passages from the Greek Testament, carefully arranged under various headings, *Faith, Promises, The Heavenly Life.* To these are added selections from Charles Wesley's hymns, then recently published, now, and for a long time past, known and prized by the devout of every communion.

But the most personal and characteristic portions of the book are Fletcher's own meditations, resolutions, and precepts. . They are written, for the most part, in Latin and in French. Some specimens of these will be found in the appendix to this volume. Here it must suffice to translate a few of the rules by which he disciplined his daily life.

Under the date January 15th, 1757, is written, in French,—

" Pray on my knees as often as possible.

Sing frequently penitential hymns.

Eat slowly, and upon my knees, three times a day only, and never more.

Always speak gently.

Neglect no outward duty.

Beware of a fire that thou kindlest thyself.

The fire that God kindles is bright, mild, constant, and burns night and day.

Think always of death, and the Cross, the hardness
of thy heart and the blood of Christ.

Beware of relaxing, and of impatience; God is faithful, but He owes thee nothing.

Speak only when necessary.

Do not surrender thyself to any joy.

Rise in the morning without yielding to sloth.

Follow always thy first motion.

Be a true son of affliction.

Write down every evening whether thou hast kept
these rules."

Among the Latin meditations is one headed "Deus
mihi amandus est quid": "God is to be loved because—"
And then follow various grounds for gratitude and love :

" Because He created me,

Of sound body and mind,

In a middle station of life, and in the bosom of His
Church ;

⁃ Preserves me alive and well ;

Has not given me over to the power of the devil ;

Gives all things necessary for life ;

In various ways, and wonderfully, has delivered me
from death ;

Raised up for me good parents, teachers, friends ;

Gives me food, shelter, books, good health,
clothing, friends, and a not dishonourable name ;

Has mercifully withheld hurtful things when I
asked them ;

Before the foundations of the world determined to
give His Son for me,

And gave Him in time to flesh, infirmities, scorn,
　　sorrows, poverty, and death ;
Imparts Him to me in the word, and in the holy
　　supper."

Among the "rules for a holy life," written in English,
the following may be quoted :

"Mortify thy five senses till crucified with Christ ;
Sit at Christ's feet ; cast away thy own will ; consult
　　His at every word, morsel, motion; ask His
　　leave even in lawful actions.
Renounce thyself in all that can hinder thy union
　　with God.　Desire nought but His love.
Mortify all affection toward inward, sensible, spiri-
　　tual delights in grace ; they rather please and
　　comfort than sanctify.
The life of God consists not in high knowledge,
　　but profound meekness, holy simplicity, and
　　ardent love to God.
Receive afflictions as the best guides to perfection.
Remember always the presence of God.
Rejoice always in the will of God.
Direct all to the glory of God."

The little book from which these extracts are taken
was Fletcher's companion in his hours of private prayer
and communion with God.　It was written, not for
others, but for himself.　For a century past it has been
in safe and reverent keeping, and is now as he left it.
Its pages are worn by his touch.　With these hymns and
meditations he nourished his soul in secret.　With these

rules he loved to bind his free Christian spirit. Like other saintly men, he found that the impulses, even of the regenerate life, may not be left to themselves with entire confidence in their sufficient working. He sought to strengthen them by meditation, to sustain them by spiritual exercises and discipline; he furnished them with tests and standards, and made self-examination definite and precise. He sought perfection at once in supreme love to God, and in the minutest details of character and conduct. Let this be borne in mind in connexion with the fact that Fletcher was a leader of the Evangelical Revival, and a founder and father of Methodism. Evangelical religion has been charged with indifference to painstaking spiritual culture. Its doctrine of salvation by faith has been thought to carry with it self-confidence, familiar ways with God, and easy dealing with one's own soul. It is supposed to compensate for its insistence upon conversion, by sanctioning subsequent laxity in the matter of prayer and fasting. It is charged with spiritual shallowness, and asked why, with all its innumerable activities, it fails to produce the deeper and more disciplined devoutness of which Thomas à Kempis in the Roman, and Andrewes and Keble in the Anglican, communities are great examples.

A proper discussion of this question would require, amongst other things, an examination of the terms in which it is stated. They would be found to contain, with some truth, assumptions utterly false and misleading. Amongst these is the assumption that sanctity is not such, unless it have a certain form, diverging not

too widely from an accepted type. The Roman controversialist objects to the Church of England that it does
not exhibit notes of sanctity, "that it has no saints."
As Dr. Mozley has said, " He refuses, in a certain case,
to see and recognise the Christian type, because it does
not come before him in the Latin shape, and with the
accompaniments of intellectual grace and refinement,
which it has incorporated on its European area."[1] By
a very slight alteration in the wording of this sentence,
it would describe with equal accuracy the attitude of
those who cannot recognise sanctity which does not
come before them in the Anglican shape ; and by a
second and a third alteration, it would describe the in-
ability, here and there existing, to discern any sanctity
but that of an accepted type or favoured school. Much
of the disparagement of "Evangelical" piety is plainly
of this kind ; and the truth needs to be spoken with
regard to all these narrow and sectarian gauges of
Christian character. Amid the "diversities of ministrations and diversities of workings," there is no essential
distinction as to the so called "note of sanctity";
Eastern or Western, Anglican or Puritan, holiness is
always and essentially the same, rebuking every attempt
to fasten it to a particular type, or ignore it apart from a
particular succession.

Fletcher was an Evangelical of Evangelicals, teaching
conversion, the witness of the Spirit, and the entire
sanctification of believers. He profoundly influenced

---

[1] MOZLEY : "Theory of Development," p. 141.

the theology and general religious spirit and character of Methodism. What then is the bearing of his spiritual life and the influence of his example upon these latter? It is this: that while holiness is, in its truest, deepest aspect, the gift of God,—it is God who sanctifies as surely as it is God who justifies,—yet, alike in the pursuit and possession of holiness, the Christian is called to work together with God, in watchfulness and prayer, in self-examination and self-denial, in reading and meditation, "exercising himself unto godliness" in the many ways which Scripture enjoins and which insight and experience will suggest.

If at any time the Methodists, or Evangelical Christians generally, should let slip either of these truths; if holiness be thought of, on the one hand, as a human attainment and not a Divine gift, or, on the other, as a gift of God having no relation to personal discipline and culture,—they will at least be breaking with their best traditions, and have against them both the teaching and the example of their fathers.

This little manual of devotion, written by his own hand, and worn by long and frequent use, reveals much of the way in which Fletcher's inmost life was cultivated. Knowing that life as it was manifested in his character and conduct, we regard with deep interest the means by which it was nurtured in secret. The lovely growth of goodness had at the root of it the patient discipline here portrayed. We might have guessed as much, but here we see that it was so.

CHAPTER V.

ENTERS THE MINISTRY.

FROM this brief glance at Fletcher's habits of devotion we return to the history of his life.   He was
not destined to be a religious recluse, cultivating in
quiet places "a fugitive and cloistered virtue."   His
thirst for communion with God was equalled by his
passion for winning souls.   If the one drove him to
retirement, the other thrust him into society.   He longed
for others to possess the salvation that he had found.
On such a matter he could not be silent, and he became
a preacher almost before he knew it.   Both in personal
intercourse and in addressing assemblies, his foreign
accent and a certain winning simplicity of manner
proved very attractive ; but the hours spent alone with
God and his own soul were the secret of a power to
appeal and persuade that was well-nigh irresistible.

Naturally it was taken for granted that his proper
vocation was the ministry.   He was pressed by one and
another, and particularly by Mr. Hill, to enter holy
orders ; but his mind was not yet made up.   His
former shrinking from an office for which he felt himself
unfit was not wholly removed.   He thought it might be

better to serve God in a private and less responsible way of life ; and yet, from time to time, the work of the ministry attracted and exercised his thoughts in a manner that might be taken to indicate God's will.

In his perplexity he sought counsel from Wesley. It is not known when, or under what circumstances, he had become personally known to him, but the letter in which he asks his advice is probably the first he ever wrote to Wesley, and the tone of it suggests that personal acquaintance, if it had begun, was as yet very slight.

" TERN,

Nov. 24*th*, 1756.

REV. SIR,—

As I. look upon you as my spiritual guide, and cannot doubt of your patience to hear, and your experience to answer, a serious question proposed by any of your people, I freely lay my case before you."

[After giving an account of his early history, and more recent experience, he tells Wesley that he had been offered a title to orders, and asks,—]

" Now, sir, the question which I beg you to decide is, whether I must and can make use of that title to get into orders. For, with respect to the living, were it vacant, I have no mind to it, because I think I could preach with more fruit in my own country and in my own tongue.

" I am in suspense. On one side my heart tells me I must try, and it tells me so whenever I feel any degree of the love of God and man ; but on the other, when

I examine whether I am fit for it, I so plainly see my
want of gifts, and especially of that *soul* of all the
labours of a minister of the gospel, *love, continual,
universal, flaming love*, that my confidence disappears,
I accuse myself of pride to dare to entertain the desire
of supporting the ark of the Lord.   As I am in both
these frames successively, I must own, sir, I do not see
plainly which of the two ways before me I can take with
safety, and I shall be glad to be ruled by you.   .   .   .
I know how precious is your time; I desire no long
answer; *persist* or *forbear* will satisfy and influence, sir,

Your unworthy servant,

J. FLETCHER."

No reply to this letter has been preserved, but
there can be no doubt as to the nature of Wesley's
advice. He recommended Fletcher's being ordained;
he probably dissuaded him from returning to Switzerland, and he discouraged the notion of his settling in
a parish. He greatly desired to see Fletcher in the
itinerant work in which he himself was engaged, the
more so as his brother Charles was now withdrawing
from it.

On Sunday, March 6th, 1757, Fletcher received
deacon's orders from the Bishop of Hereford, and on
the following Sunday he was ordained priest by the
Bishop of Bangor, at the request of the Bishop of Hereford. The day after receiving priest's orders he was
licensed "to perform the office of curate in the parish
church of Madeley, in the county of Salop," and "a

yearly salary of twenty-five pounds, to be paid quarterly, for serving the same," was assigned to him.

This license to the curacy must not be confounded with his appointment, more than three years afterwards, to the vicarage of Madeley. Fletcher has no history as curate of Madeley. The appointment was in fact a nominal one, for it is tolerably certain that he exercised no spiritual function whatever in Madeley for at least two years after his ordination. The title to orders was probably given to him by the Rev. Rowland Chambre, then Vicar of Madeley, at Mr. Hill's request, with the understanding that the curacy should be only nominal. The position of chaplain and tutor in Mr. Hill's family, though not furnishing a legal title to orders, would be considered equivalent to a cure of souls. The fact that he was ordained deacon and priest on two consecutive Sundays, the customary interval of a year being dispensed with, may be ascribed either to the influence of Mr. Hill, or of Wesley himself; or it may be taken as proof that his character was admittedly high, and that in his examination or interviews with the bishop, he had shown himself exceptionally well qualified, both intellectually and morally.

His connexion with Mr. Hill's family drew to its close. It did not afford him the sphere for Christian work that he desired, and involved him in occasional embarrassments and difficulties. Mr. Hill was uniformly kind, but he feared that the scandal of Methodism attaching to his tutor would injure him at the next election. The neighbouring clergy for the most part fought shy of Fletcher, so that he had few opportunities of preaching in their churches. But the one compensation for these restrictions was found in the devout retirement he loved so well. He writes to Wesley : "The will of God be done : I am in His hands ; and if He does not call me to so much public duty, I have the more time for study, prayer, and praise." He seems to have been conscious that it was a time of discipline and preparation with him, and until the indications of God's will were plain, he would not seek release from a position where the providence of God had placed him.

Meanwhile, as his tutorship became less and less satisfactory as a vocation, his connexion with the Methodists opened up to him new labours and new friendships. Immediately upon his ordination Fletcher was drawn into the full stream of the Revival, and brought into active association with its leaders. His very first ministerial act, on the day that he was ordained priest, was to assist Wesley in the administration of the Lord's supper at Snowsfields chapel ; and from that time he frequently read prayers and preached in the Methodist chapels in London. He made the acquaintance of Charles Wesley and Whitefield, of the Countess of Huntingdon, of Berridge, Vicar of Everton, of Thomas Walsh, and of some of the devout women who were not least among the glories of early Methodism, including Mary Bosanquet, who, many years afterwards, became his wife. By these and others Fletcher was received with no common welcome. Wesley himself wrote in his "Journal," "When my bodily strength failed, and none in England were able and willing to assist me, He sent me help from the mountains of Switzerland, and a helpmeet for me in every respect; where could I find such another?" A little later the Countess of Huntingdon wrote to a friend: "I have seen Mr. Fletcher, and was both pleased and refreshed by the interview. He was accompanied by Mr. Wesley, who had frequently mentioned him in terms of high commendation, as had Mr. Whitefield, Mr. Charles Wesley, and others, so that I was anxious to become acquainted with one so devoted, and who appears to glory in nothing, save in the Cross of our Divine Lord and Master."

Another testimony referring to this time, though written many years later, is that of a Mrs. Crosby, well-known amongst the first Methodists: "I heard this heavenly-minded servant of the Lord preach his first sermon in West Street chapel. I think his text was, 'Repent: for the kingdom of heaven is at hand.' His spirit appeared in his whole attitude and action. He could not well find words in the English language to express himself, but he supplied that defect by offering up prayers, tears, and sighs."

Of all those with whom Fletcher was now brought into close and happy relations, Charles Wesley seems to have most completely won his heart. Towards the elder Wesley he showed affectionate reverence, and a loyalty that had its trials, and gave its proofs in many ways. He undoubtedly looked upon him as the chief of living men. Of Thomas Walsh, whose life, Southey says, "might almost convince a Catholic that saints are to be

E

found in other communions, as well as in the Church of
Rome,"—of Walsh, Fletcher, impressed with his deep,
stern, mystic sanctity, wrote, "I wish I could attend him
everywhere, as Elisha attended Elijah." But it was in
Charles Wesley that he found his dearest and most intimate friend, to whom for years he turned for solace, for
counsel, and for confidential intercourse.

We have seen the terms in which Lady Huntingdon
speaks of Fletcher after her first interview with him.
On his part, Fletcher was profoundly impressed with the
countess's manifold excellences, and wrote to Charles
Wesley that he had "passed three hours with a modern
prodigy—*a humble and pious countess.*" Lady Huntingdon has perhaps suffered in the modern estimate of
her character and work from the overstrained and even
fulsome language concerning her which it was the
custom of many of her friends and followers to employ.
Appreciation of her ladyship's rank so mingled with
esteem for her piety as to produce an unhappy effect
upon the phraseology of her admirers. The countess's
biographer continues, in a later age, a style which, barely
endurable when a century old, is intolerable when repeated and renewed. He speaks of "the elegant and
pious persons to whom Mr. Fletcher was invited to
preach and administer the sacrament"! But we must
not allow the effusive language of her contemporaries,
or the fine writing of her biographer, to conceal from us
the true worth of a very able and most devoted Christian
woman. If that language seem to us occasionally wanting in manliness, in proper self-respect, and in Christian

simplicity, it bears witness to the ascendency exercised by a remarkable character over all but the very strongest of those who came under its influence ; and if it was dangerous to be the subject of so much eulogy, it should be remembered that Lady Huntingdon never shrank from running counter to the prejudices of the class to which she belonged, and endured, for the sake of Christ and His cause, ridicule from those of her own order, which most people would find harder to bear than actual persecution.

Fletcher was added to the number of Lady Huntingdon's chaplains. It is almost unnecessary to say that this was not an "appointment" in the strict sense of the word, but that he preached from time to time to the fashionable congregations that assembled at Lady Huntingdon's house at Chelsea. These assemblies have often been described. They included the most distinguished men and women of the day. Chesterfield, Bolingbroke, Horace Walpole and others, bear witness to the fashion which prevailed. To listen to Whitefield in Lady Huntingdon's drawing-room became a recognised diversion for society, and the most cynical and worldly were found side by side with the serious and devout. Undoubtedly some "who came to scoff remained to pray." Amongst the women of rank who heard the gospel in this way several were converted, and became earnest and faithful witnesses for Christ ; but the hindrances to deep and lasting results were very great, and we are inclined to think that this particular phase of the Evangelical Revival was by no means

among its most fruitful or important developments.
The ignorance and brutality of the crowds to whom
Wesley and Whitefield preached, presented no such
resistance to the gospel as the vanity and finished worldliness of the drawing-room congregations. An instance
will suffice. A lady who had been invited by Lady
Huntingdon replied in the following terms: "I thank
your ladyship for the information concerning the
Methodist preachers. Their doctrines are most repul-
sive, and strongly tinctured with impertinence and dis-
respect towards their superiors, in perpetually endeavour-
ing to level all ranks and do away with all distinctions.
It is monstrous to be told you have a heart as sinful as
the common wretches that crawl on the earth. This is
highly offensive and insulting, and I cannot but wonder
that your ladyship should relish any sentiments so much
at variance with high rank and good breeding."[1]

There is no record of the impression made by
Fletcher upon these fashionable congregations. Meanwhile he was engaged in a work probably more con-
genial to him, viz. preaching to the French prisoners, a
number of whom were settled at Tunbridge. After a
few months this came to an end; he was forbidden
by the Bishop of London to continue his ministrations.
There was something "irregular" in them, it would
appear. Wesley wrote afterwards, "If I had known this
at the time, King George should have known it; and I
believe he would have given the bishop little thanks."

---

[1] GLEDSTONE: "Life of Whitefield," p. 304.

The following extracts from his letters belong to this period :

· To the Rev. Charles Wesley.

"*Mar. 22nd*, 1759.

Since your departure I have lived more than ever like a hermit. It seems to me that I am an unprofit-able weight upon the earth. I want to hide myself from all. I tremble when the Lord favours me with a sight of myself. I tremble to think of preaching only to dis-honour God. To-morrow I preach at West Street, with all the feelings of Jonah. Oh! would to God I might be attended with success! If the Lord shall in any degree sustain my weakness, I shall consider myself as indebted to your prayers.

"A proposal has lately been made to me to accom-pany Mr. Nathanael Gilbert to the West Indies. I have weighed the matter; but, on the one hand, I feel that I have neither zeal nor grace nor talents to expose myself to the temptations and labours of a mission to the West Indies; and, on the other, I believe that if God call me thither the time is not yet come. . . . Pray let me know what you think of this business; if you con-demn me to put the sea between us, the command would be a hard one, but I might possibly prevail on myself to give you that proof of the deference I pay to your judicious advice. Give me some account of Mrs. Wesley, and of the godfather she designs for your little Charles; and, that she may not labour under a decep-tion, tell her how greatly I want wisdom, and add that I have no more grace than wisdom. If, after all, she

will not reject so unworthy a sponsor, remember that I
have taken you for a father and adviser, and that the
charge will in the end devolve upon you.   Adieu !"

To the Same.

"*April,* 1759.

" I have lately seen so much weakness in my heart,
both as a minister and a Christian, that I know not
which is most to be pitied, the man, the believer, or the
preacher.   Could I at last be truly humbled, and continue so always, I should esteem myself happy in making
this discovery.   I preach merely to keep the chapel
open until God shall send a workman after His own
heart.   *Nos numeri sumus*—this is almost all I can say
of myself."

To the Same.

"*Nov.* 15*th,* 1759.

"The countess proposed to me something of what
you hinted to me in your garden, namely, to celebrate
the Communion sometimes at her house in a morning,
and to preach when occasion offered ; in such a manner
however as not to restrain my liberty, nor to prevent
my assisting you, or preaching to the French refugees ;
and that only till Providence should clearly point out
the path in which I should go.   Charity, politeness, and
reason accompanied her offer, and I confess, in spite
of the resolution which I had almost absolutely formed,
to fly the houses of the great, without even the exception
of the countess's, I found myself so greatly changed that
I should have accepted on the spot a proposal which I

should have declined from any other mouth; but my engagement with you withheld me, and, thanking the countess, I told her, when I had reflected on her obliging offer, I would do myself the honour of waiting upon her again.

"Nevertheless, two difficulties stand in my way. Will it be consistent with that poverty of spirit which I seek? Can I accept an office for which I have such small talents? And shall I not dishonour the cause of God by stammering out the mysteries of the gospel in a place where the most approved ministers of the Lord have preached with so much power and so much success? I suspect that my own vanity gives more weight to this second objection than it deserves to have : what think you? You are an indulgent father to me, and the name of son suits me better than that of brother." [1]

---

[1] An expression in one of Fletcher's letters to Charles Wesley, written in 1759, is noteworthy in connexion with the ecclesiastical development of Methodism. He speaks of "the Methodist Church." Is not this the earliest instance of the use of this term?

CHAPTER VI

*FIRST YEARS AT MADELEY.—DIFFICULTIES AND
DISCOURAGEMENTS.*

(1760–1767.)

FLETCHER had now completed his thirty-first year, and had been three years and a half in orders. Ten years had elapsed since his coming to England, and he had no thought of returning to Switzerland. The anglicised form of his name was significant of the change that had taken place in his sentiments and sympathics. In these he had become an Englishman, although—and it is necessary to mark the distinction—his *temperament* was never naturalised, but remained that of a foreigner to the last. The yearning for his native land, which is supposed to characterise the Swiss, was wholly wanting in him. Spiritual affections and aspirations seemed to leave little room for love of country, and, for a time at least, to dissolve the ties of family and home. On this subject Charles Wesley, as we gather from a letter of Fletcher's, administered a mild reproof, to which he replies, with the utmost simplicity, that he had often thought "that the particular fault of the Swiss is to be without natural affection." It should be added that later years showed that he had no need to seek shelter under any such doubtful generalization, or charge himself with so grievous a moral deficiency.

Meanwhile, his position needed defining to himself, and to others. He was not adequately or satisfactorily employed. His labours in connexion with the Wesleys and Lady Huntingdon, broken off and resumed from time to time, according as he lived in London or in Shropshire, were but preparatory to some more definite and continuous vocation. What that should be he knew not. It was however soon to be determined.

His friend Mr. Hill, desirous of doing something for the tutor of his sons, offered him the living of Dunham, in Cheshire. "The parish," said he, "is small, the duty light, the income good (£400 per annum), and it is situated in a fine, healthy, sporting country." "Alas!" replied Fletcher, "Dunham will not suit me; there is too much money and too little labour." All that Mr. Hill could say to this unexpected difficulty was, "Few clergymen make such objections," and to tell him that it was a pity to decline such a living, as he did not know where he could find him another. What was to be done? Mr. Hill suggested Madeley; "Would you like that?" "That, sir," said Fletcher, "would be the very place for me." "My object," answered Mr. Hill, "is to make you comfortable in your own way. If you prefer Madeley, I shall find no difficulty in persuading Mr. Chambre to exchange it for Dunham, which is worth more than twice as much as Madeley." A nephew of Mr. Hill was patron of Madeley, and the uncle and nephew meeting soon after at Shrewsbury races, the exchange of livings was negotiated then and there, and the result communicated to Fletcher. On his part there were still a few doubts and heart-searchings, and one powerful influence was opposed to his accepting this or any other living: Wesley wanted him for itinerant work, and told him, " Others may do well in a living ; you cannot, it is not your calling." " I tell him," says Fletcher, " I readily own that I am not fit to plant or water any part of the Lord's vineyard ; but that *if* I am called at all, I am called to preach at Madeley, where I was first sent into the ministry, and where a chain of providences I could not break has again fastened me."

With these convictions the matter was soon settled. His induction to " the vicarage of the parish church of Madeley " was signed by the Bishop of Hereford, on October 4th, 1760. Henceforth Fletcher is Vicar of Madeley. He has found the sphere of labour where he was to spend the remainder of his days, and received the designation by which he will ever be remembered.[1]

---

[1] I am indebted to the Rev. George Mather for the opportunity of examining the documents relating to Fletcher's ordination, license, induction, &c. They are as follows :

1. Deacon's orders, March 6th, 1757, Bishop of Hereford.
2. Priest's orders, March 13th, 1757, Bishop of Bangor.
3. License to the curacy of Madeley, March 14th, 1757, Bishop of Hereford.
4. Presentation to vicarage of Madeley, October 4th, 1760.
5. Institution to vicarage of Madeley, October 7th, 1760.
6. Mandate for induction, October 7th, 1760.
7. Certificate of Fletcher's conforming to the Liturgy, October 7th, 1760.

Among the country parishes of England are many whose remoteness from toil and din, and tranquil beauty of church and parsonage, of hall and cottage, have made them meet homes for gentle-spirited men. George Herbert at Bemerton, Augustus Hare at Alton, John Keble at Hursley, represent an element in the historic Church of England, which is to its more imposing aspects what the pastoral scenery amid which they lived, is to the mountains of Westmorland or Wales. Had the providence which shaped Fletcher's course guided him to some such retirement, and made him shepherd of a simple, docile flock, no man would have trodden with greater meekness and fidelity the quiet ways of the country parson ; but he was called to another and more arduous service. Few scenes of labour could be less attractive, considered in itself, than that upon which he was now entering. The parish of Madeley, including Coalbrookdale and Madeley Wood, was large and populous. The inhabitants were principally colliers and ironworkers, ignorant, rough, and brutal. Their condition is not to be wondered at. Little or nothing had been done to raise and improve them. The well-organized,

---

8. Certificate of subscribing to the Thirty-nine Articles, October 7th, 1760.

9. Certificate, signed by two parishioners, stating that on Lord's day, October 26th, 1760, John Fletcher, Vicar of Madeley, had read prayers, and declared his unfeigned assent and consent, &c., dated December 1st, 1760.

These documents are all in good condition, and the signatures perfectly fresh and clear.

well-worked parish of modern times, was not yet in
existence. The non-residence of the clergy, which lasted
throughout the century, as may be seen by the language
of Bishop Burnet at its beginning and of Bishop Horsley
at its close, was a fruitful source of many evils, and a
chief hindrance in the way of a higher standard of parochial duty. Another twenty years was to elapse before
any serious attempt was made to establish Sunday
schools. Public catechizing had fallen into disuse.
Day schools were few and inefficient. Voluntary
associations for Christian work were all but unknown.
The district visitor, the tract distributer, the Bible-
woman, the home missionary, the many organizations of
Christian piety and zeal with which the land is now
covered, had not yet arisen. The Revival was to
produce them in due course, but meanwhile the mass of
the people was untouched by any effectual Christian
influences, save where the Methodist clergy, or Wesley's
itinerants, brought the gospel home to them. What
could be expected of a rough collier population but hard
drinking, profane swearing, and cruel sports? These
were common practices everywhere, and were not likely
to be found in their mildest forms among the people of
Madeley and the neighbouring villages.

In his letters to Charles Wesley and the Countess of
Huntingdon, Fletcher gives some particulars respecting
his parish and the work he had undertaken.

"*Oct.* 28*th*, 1760.

"I preached last Sunday for the first time in my

church, and shall continue to do so, though I propose
staying with Mr. Hill till he leaves the country, which
will be, I suppose, in a fortnight, partly to comply with
him to the last, partly to avoid falling out with my pre-
decessor, who is still at Madeley, but who will remove
about the same time."

"*Nov.* 19*th*, 1760.

" I have hitherto wrote my sermons, but am carried so
far beyond my notes when in the pulpit that I purpose
preaching with only my sermon-case in my hand next
Friday, when I shall venture on an evening lecture for
the first time. I question whether I shall have above
half a dozen hearers, as the god of a busy world is
doubly the god of this part of the world, but I am
resolved to try. The weather and the roads are so bad
that the way to the church is almost impracticable;
nevertheless all the seats were full last Sunday. I
cannot yet discern any deep work, or indeed anything
but what will always attend the crying down man's
righteousness, and insisting upon Christ's,—I mean a
general liking among the poor, and offence, ridicule, and
opposition among the ' reputable ' and ' wise ' people.
Should the Lord vouchsafe to plant the gospel in this
country, my parish seems to be the best spot for the
centre of a work, as it lies just among the most populous,
profane, and ignorant."

"*Jan.* 6*th*, 1761.

" As to my parish, all that I see hitherto in it is nothing but what one may expect from speaking plainly
and with some degree of earnestness : a crying out, ' He's

a Methodist, a downright Methodist'; while some of the poorer sort say, 'nay, but he speaketh the truth.' Some of the best farmers and most respectable tradesmen talk often among themselves (as I am told) about turning me out of my living as a Methodist or a Baptist. . . . My Friday lecture took better than I expected, and I propose to continue it till the congregation desert me. . . . The number of communicants is increased from thirty to above a hundred; and a few seem to seek grace in the means."

"April 27th, 1761.

"Last Sunday I had the pleasure of seeing some in the churchyard who could not get into the church. I began a few Sundays ago to preach in the afternoon, after catechising the children, but I do not preach my own sermons. Twice I read a sermon of Archbishop Ussher, and last Sunday one of the homilies, taking the liberty to make some observations on such passages as confirmed what I advanced in the morning; and by this means I stopped the mouths of many adversaries. . . . You will do well to engage your colliers at Kingswood to pray for their poor brethren at Madeley. May those at Madeley one day equal them *in faith,* as they *now do* in that wickedness for which they (the Kingswood colliers) were famous before you went among them."

"Aug. 12th, 1761.

"I know not what to say to you of the state of my soul. I daily struggle in the Slough of Despond, and I endeavour every day to climb the hill Difficulty. I need wisdom, mildness, and courage : and no man has less of them than I. O Jesus, my Saviour, draw me strongly to Him who giveth wisdom to all who ask it, and upbraideth them not ! As to the state of my parish, the prospect is yet discouraging. New scandals succeed those that wear away. But offences must come. Happy shall I be if the offence cometh not by me ! My church-wardens speak of hindering strangers from coming to the church, and of repelling them from the Lord's table; but on these points I am determined to make head against them. A club of eighty workmen in a neighbouring parish, being offended at their minister, determined to come in procession to my church, and requested me to preach a sermon for them ; but I thought proper to decline it, and have thereby a little regained the good graces of the minister, at least for a time."

"*Oct.* 12*th,* 1761.

" Discouragements follow one after another with very little intermission. Those which are of an inward nature are sufficiently known to you ; but some others are peculiar to myself, especially those I have had for eight days past, during Madeley wake. Seeing that I could not suppress these bacchanals, I did all in my power to moderate their madness ; but my endeavours have had little or no effect. You cannot well imagine how much the animosity of my parishioners is heightened, and with what boldness it discovers itself against me, because I preached against drunkenness, shows, and bull-baiting. The publicans and maltmen will not forgive me; they think that to preach against drunkenness and to cut their purse is the same thing."

Fletcher's difficulties during these earlier years at Madeley were, indeed, very numerous. In his letters he passes lightly over the violence of the more ignorant and brutal of his flock. Though from time to time dangerous enough, it did not daunt or distress him so much as some other kinds of opposition. While fearlessly reproving their vices, he was full of tenderness and pity for the poor sinful wretches who cursed and insulted him to his face. He sought them separately, literally pursuing those who tried to hide themselves from him, and entreated them to turn from their sins. He would break in upon their assemblies, where drunkenness and obscenity had scarcely any limits, and reprove them with an earnestness that touched the consciences of some, while it roused others to resentment and revenge. On one occasion at least he had a narrow escape for his life. One Sunday evening when he was expected at Madeley Wood, a number of colliers, who were baiting a bull, maddened with drink and excitement, agreed *to bait the parson.* Some of them undertook to pull him off his horse as soon as he appeared, while the rest were to set the dogs upon him. But the providence of God prevented this crime, and protected the faithful minister. Just as he was about to set out for Madeley Wood he was unexpectedly sent for to bury a child, and so was detained until it was too late to go to the Wood; and the drunken colliers, who were cursing their ill luck, had nothing for it but to return to the public-house and solace themselves after their manner.

From among the very worst of these despisers of his ministry some, however, were converted to God, and became his joy and consolation.

On a certain Sunday, after reading prayers at Madeley, he says that his mind became so confused that he could not recollect his text or any part of his sermon. Under these circumstances he began to explain and apply the first lesson, which was the third chapter of the Book of Daniel, containing the account of Shadrach, Meshach, and Abednego being cast into the fiery furnace. The remainder of the story may be told in Fletcher's own words. "I found in doing this such extraordinary assistance from God, and such a peculiar enlargement of heart, that I supposed there must be some peculiar cause for it. I therefore desired, if any of the congregation found anything particular, they would acquaint me with it in the ensuing week. In conse-quence of this, the Wednesday after a woman came and gave the following account :

"'I have been for some time much concerned about my soul. I have attended church at all opportunities, and have spent much time in private prayer. At this my husband, who is a butcher, has been exceedingly enraged, and has threatened me severely as to what he would do to me if I did not leave off going to John Fletcher's church; yea, if I dared to go again to any religious meetings whatever. When I told him I could not in conscience refrain from going, at least

F

to the parish church, he became outrageous, and swore dreadfully, and said if I went again he would cut my throat as soon as I came back. This made me cry to God that He would support me; and though I did not feel any great degree of comfort, yet, having a sure confidence in God, I determined to do my duty, and leave the event to Him. Last Sunday, after many struggles with the devil and my own heart, I came downstairs ready for church. My husband said he should not cut my throat, as he had intended, but he would heat the oven, and throw me into it the moment I came home. Notwithstanding this threat, which he enforced with many bitter oaths, I went to church, praying all the way that God would strengthen me to suffer whatever might befall me. While you were speaking of the three children whom Nebuchadnezzar cast into the burning, fiery furnace, I found all you said belonged to me. God applied every word to my heart; and when the sermon was ended I thought if I had a thousand lives I could lay them all down for Him. I felt so filled with His love that I hastened home, fully determined to give myself to whatsoever God pleased, nothing doubting that He either would take me to heaven, if He suffered me to be burnt to death, or that He would in some way deliver me, as He did His three servants that trusted in Him. When I got to my own door I saw flames issuing from the oven, and I expected to be thrown into it immediately. I felt my heart rejoice that if it were so the will of the Lord would be done. I opened the door, and to my astonishment saw my husband upon his knees, praying for the forgiveness of his sins. He caught me in his arms, earnestly begged my pardon, and has continued diligently seeking God ever since.' "

But there was opposition, as has been said, that weighed more heavily upon Fletcher's spirit than that of the poor and ignorant, who knew not what they did. Now it was a "new convert, whom the devil had by fifty visions set on the pinnacle of the temple. I have had more trouble with her visions than with her unbelief." Then he writes : " A daughter of one of my most substantial parishioners, giving place to Satan by pride and impatience, is driven in her conviction into a kind of madness. Judge how our adversaries rejoiced !"

Another incident caused him almost to despair of any good. A constable was sent to his house upon information that a cry of murder had been heard there on Christmas Day. The report arose from the cries from a young woman, who used to fall into convulsions, sometimes in the church and sometimes in the private meetings. He writes: " Her constitution is considerably weakened as well as her understanding. What to do in this case I know not ; for those who are tempted in this manner pay as little regard to reason as the miserable people in Bedlam." He adds, " And for my part I was tempted to forsake my ministry and take to my heels."

A further affliction was the ill-will of the neighbouring clergy and gentry. At the archdeacon's visitation

a sermon was preached against what were called the
"doctrines of Methodism," and after the sermon
Fletcher was triumphantly asked what answer he could
make.   A young clergyman, living in Madeley Wood,
fastened a paper to the door of the parish church
charging him with "rebellion, schism, and being a
disturber of the public peace."   He had opened a
room for religious services in a small house built upon
the rock in Madeley Wood.   Hence it was known as
the Rock Church.   It was determined to put the Con-
venticle Act in force against him.   A poor widow who
lived in the house, Mary Matthews by name, and a
young man who used to take part in the services held
there, were arrested and taken before the justice.
Mary Matthews was fined £20, and the justice proposed to grant a warrant for the apprehension of
Fletcher.   The other justices thinking it a matter
beyond their jurisdiction, the warrant was not issued.
His churchwardens talked loudly of putting him in the
spiritual court for holding meetings in houses, and,
Fletcher adds, "what is worse than all, three false
witnesses offer to prove upon oath that I am a liar;
and some of '*my followers*' (as they are called) have
dishonoured their profession, to the great joy of our
adversaries."

No wonder he was from time to time greatly cast
down.   His health was delicate, he lived alone, and,
between deliberate fasting and unconscious neglect of himself, his body suffered and his spirits were depressed.
He writes to Charles Wesley : "I preach, I exhort, I

pray, etc., but as yet I seem to have cast the net on the
wrong side of the ship. Lord Jesus, come Thyself and
furnish me with a Divine commission! For some
months past I have laboured under an insufferable drowsiness. I could sleep day and night, and the hours which
I ought to employ with Christ on the mountain I spend
like Peter in the garden."

The drowsiness of which he complains was probably
connected with what Wesley says was his invariable
rule; viz. to sit up two whole nights in a week, and
devote the time to reading, meditation, and prayer.
We have seen that Wesley disapproved these austerities
as "well intended but not well judged." It would
be easy, but ungracious, to expand into censure what
Wesley so gently touched upon. It will be pleasanter
to look for a moment upon the solitary vicar at his
frugal meal, as portrayed by one who never forgot her
girlish visit to the vicarage.

"Mr. Fletcher sometimes visited a boarding school
at Madeley. One morning he came in just as the
girls had sat down to breakfast. He said but little
while the meal lasted, but when it was finished he
spoke to each girl separately, and concluded by saying
to the whole, 'I have waited some time on you this
morning, that I might see you eat your breakfast; and
I hope you will visit me to-morrow morning and see
how I eat mine.' He told them his breakfast hour
was seven o'clock, and obtained a promise that they
would visit him. Next morning they went at the time
appointed, and seated themselves in the kitchen.

Mr. Fletcher came in, quite rejoiced to see them. On the table stood a small basin of milk and sops of bread. Mr. Fletcher took the basin across the kitchen, and sat down on an old bench. He then took out his watch, laid it before him, and said : ' My dear girls, yesterday morning I waited on you a full hour while you were at breakfast. I shall take as much time this morning in eating my breakfast as I usually do, if not rather more. Look at my watch! and he immediately began to eat and continued in conversation with them. When he had finished he asked them how long he had been at breakfast. They said, ' Just a minute and a half, sir.' ' Now, my dear girls,' said he, ' we have fifty-eight minutes of the hour left '; and he began to sing—

> ' Our life is a dream ;
> Our time as a stream
> Glides swiftly away,
> And the fugitive moment refuses to stay.' "

After this he gave them a lecture on the value of time, and the worth of the soul. They then all knelt down in prayer, after which he dismissed them with impressions on the mind the narrator never ceased to remember.[1]

In following Fletcher through the earlier years of his

---

[1] Published in a sermon preached on the occasion of the death of Fletcher's widow in 1816, by the Rev. John Hodson, who had the incident from "a pious woman who for many years was intimately acquainted with Mr. Fletcher." Quoted from Tyerman's " Life of Fletcher."

ministry at Madeley the thought will present itself to
most persons that a good wife would have been an in-
calculable blessing to him. In a letter to Mr. Perronet,
written in November, 1765, he says, "I live alone in
my house, having neither wife, child, nor servant."
Surely this is a somewhat forlorn view of the Vicar of
Madeley, which not all his gentle cheerfulness can
effectually brighten. A wife's ministering would have
been as good for his health and comfort as her sympathy
and counsel would have been helpful in the peculiar
difficulties of his pastorate. George Herbert, in his
" Country Parson," though he shows a sufficient leaning
towards the celibacy of the clergy, yet qualifies his
verdict : " The country parson, considering that virginity
is a higher state than matrimony, and that the ministry
requires the best and highest thing, is rather unmarried
than married. But yet, . . . as the temper of his
parish may be, where he may have occasion to converse
with women, and that amongst suspicious men, and
other like circumstances considered, he is rather married
than unmarried." Fletcher was never suspected of
levity or indiscretion. It was hardly within the power,
either of the foolish or the malicious, to fasten scandal
upon one so transparently pure in spirit and demeanour.
But, as it has been seen, the religious fears and fancies,
and morbid or fanatical conditions of certain women
caused him much trouble, and almost made him despair
of his work. In these matters the aid of such a wife as
Fletcher would have married—as many years afterwards
he did marry—would have been invaluable. It is the

more to be regretted that he did not marry, as it appears that his heart was already drawn towards Miss Bosanquet, his future wife. But her fortune he regarded as an almost insuperable obstacle. Juvenal's sarcasm, *Veniunt a dote sagittæ*, recurred to him, and he shrank from the notion of becoming the suitor of a wealthy woman. Charles Wesley thought it would be better for him to marry; but he repelled the suggestion, and wrote him several "reasons against matrimony," which, to say the truth, are a very laboured piece of writing, and are never likely to convince any human being whose mind is not already made up.

CHAPTER VII

CONTROVERSY AND CORRESPONDENCE.

ALMOST from the beginning of his ministry Fletcher's pen was active in the service of religion. From various causes much, if not the greater part, of his writings was controversial, and to this fact may be assigned, in part at least, their immediate popularity and subsequent neglect. But the spirit of controversy never got the better of the spirit of devotion. Whatever view may be taken of the Calvinist controversy, in which he took a leading part, few will dissent from Southey's judgment: " If ever true Christian charity was manifested in polemical writing, it was by Fletcher of Madeley. Even theological controversy never in the slightest degree irritated his heavenly temper." Some extracts from his earlier writings will show the spirit in which he entered upon this part of his labours.

In reply to the visitation sermon attacking the "doctrines of Methodism," he wrote, in July, 1761, a short "Defence of Experimental Religion," which may be classed amongst the best apologies of the period. He had now acquired an easy, pleasant English style, tending somewhat to the florid and diffuse, but generally

stopping short of excess, and often forcible and persuasive in a high degree.   He had no difficulty in
showing that to represent virtue and morality as the way
to salvation is neither agreeable to the Scripture nor
to the doctrine of the Church of England.   The true
nature of justification, and of the faith that justifies, he
illustrates from the Articles and Homilies.   The necessity of God's grace to turn the will, as against the
superficial notion that a man is as free to do good as
to do evil, is shown from Article X., from the baptismal
office, and the collect for Ash Wednesday.

It was inevitable in the state of religion in England,
and considering the chief intellectual influences then in
the ascendant, that to preach salvation as a present
blessing to be possessed and enjoyed, was to incur the
charge of enthusiasm.   The high and moderate clergy
never felt surer of themselves than when exposing the
folly and presumption of " feelings " and " experiences "
in religion.   Fletcher distinguishes between what is true
and what is false on this subject :

"To set up impulses as the standard of our faith or
rule of our conduct; to take the thrilling of weak nerves,
sinking of the animal spirits, or flights of a heated
imagination, for the workings of God's Spirit ; to pretend
to miraculous gifts, and those fruits of the Spirit which
are not offered and promised to believers in all ages,
or to boast of the graces which that Spirit produces in
the heart of every child of God, when the fruits of the
flesh appear in our life—this is downright enthusiasm :
I detest it as well as you, sir, and I heartily wish you

good luck whenever you shall attack such monstrous
delusions.

" But is it consistent with the doctrines of our Church
to condemn and set aside all *feelings* in religion, and
rank them with unaccountable *impulses?* Give me
leave, sir, to tell you that either you or the compilers
of our Liturgy, Articles, and Homilies must be mistaken, if I did not mistake you. . . . They bid us
pray (office for the sick) that every sick person may
know and feel that there is no saving name or power
but that of Jesus Christ. In the seventeenth of our
Articles they speak of godly persons, and such as *feel*
in themselves the workings of God's Spirit. And in
the third part of the homily for rogation week, they
declare that when after contrition we *feel* our consciences
at peace with God through the remission of our sin, it
is God that worketh this miracle in us. (Compare this
with Rom. v. 1.) They are so far therefore from at-
tributing such *feelings* to the weakness of good people's
nerves, or to a spirit of pride and delusion, that they
affirm it is God that worketh them in their hearts. . . .

" You seemed, sir, to discountenance *feelings* as not
agreeable to sober, rational worship ; but, if I am not
mistaken, reason by no means clashes with feelings of
various sorts in religion. I am willing to let any man
of reason judge whether feeling sorrow for sin, hunger
and thirst after righteousness, peace of conscience,
serenity of mind, consolation in prayer, thankfulness
at the Lord's table, hatred of sin, zeal for God, love
to Jesus and all men, compassion for the distressed, etc.,

or feeling nothing at all of this, is matter of mere indifference : yea, sir, take for a judge a heathen poet, if
you please, and you will hear him say of a young man
who, by his blushes, betrayed the shame he felt for
having told an untruth,—*Erubuit, salva res est.*   .   .

"If a man may feel sorrow when he sees himself stript
of all, and left naked upon a desert coast, why should
not a penitent sinner, whom God has delivered from
blindness of heart, be allowed to feel sorrow upon
seeing himself robbed of his title to heaven, and left
in the wilderness of this world destitute of original
righteousness ?   Again, if it is not absurd to say that a
rebel, condemned to death, feels joy upon his being
reprieved and received into his prince's favour, why
should it be thought absurd to affirm that a Christian,
who, being justified by faith, has peace with God, and
rejoices in hope of the glory to come, feels joy and
happiness in his inmost soul on that account ?   On the
contrary, sir, to affirm that such a one feels nothing
(if I am not mistaken) is no less repugnant to reason
than to religion.   .   .   .

"But if, because your text was taken out of St. Paul's
epistle, you choose, sir, to let him decide whether feelings ought to have place in sound religion, or not, I am
willing to stand at the bar before so great a judge, and
promise to find no fault with his sentence.   .   .
Where does he exclaim against feeling the power of
God, or the powerful operations of His Spirit on the
heart ?   Is it where he says that the kingdom of God is
'not in word, but in power '; that this kingdom within

us (if we are believers), this true, inward religion consists in peace, righteousness, and joy in the Holy Ghost; that Christians rejoice in tribulation, because the love of God is shed abroad in their hearts by the Holy Ghost given unto them? Is it where he says, he is 'not ashamed of the gospel of Christ, because it is the power of God to the salvation of every one that believeth'; that he desired to 'know nothing but Jesus and the power of His resurrection'? (2 Cor. ii. 24.) Or is it when he calls the exerting of this power in him his life; saying, 'I live not, but Christ lives in me; and the life that I now live in the flesh, I live by the faith of the Son of God, who loved me and gave Himself for me'?

"Can we suppose that he discountenances feelings in religion, when he prays that 'the God of hope' would fill the Romans (xv. 13) 'with all joy and peace in believing, that they might abound in hope through the power of the Holy Ghost'; when he says that 'they had not received again the spirit of bondage to fear, but the spirit of adoption, crying, Abba, Father, and witnessing to their spirits that they were the children of God,' agreeable to that of St. John, 'He that believeth hath the witness in himself'?

"One more argument on this subject, and I shall conclude the whole. If good nature, affability, and morality, with a round of outward duties, will fit a man for heaven, without any feeling of the workings of the Spirit of God in the heart, or without peace, righteousness, and joy in the Holy Ghost; if such a professor of

godliness is really in that narrow way to the kingdom
which few people find, why did our Lord puzzle honest
Nicodemus with the strange doctrine of a new birth?
. . . why did He trouble the religious centurion
with sending for Peter, that the Holy Ghost might fall
upon him and all that heard the word, while the apostle
preached to them remission of sins, through faith in
Jesus?

"But, above all, if inward feelings are nothing in
sound religion, if they rather border upon enthusiasm,
why did not our Lord caution the woman who came
behind him in Simon's house, who wept at his feet, and
kissed and wiped them with her hair? Why did He
not take this opportunity to preach her and us a lecture
on enthusiasm? Why did He not advise her to take
something to help the weakness of her nerves, and
prevent the ferment of her spirits? Why did He not
tell her she went too far, she would run mad in the end?
Why did He not bid her (as people do in our days) go
into company a little, and divert her melancholy? Nay,
more; why did He prefer her with all her behaviour to
good-natured, virtuous, religious, undisturbed Simon?

". . . However, do not mistake me, sir; I am
far from supposing that the sincerity of people's devotion must be judged of by the emotion they feel in their
bodies. . . . But as I read that God will have the
heart or nothing, so I know that when He has the heart,
He has the affections, of course. Fear and hope,
sorrow and joy, desire and love act upon their proper
objects, God's attributes. They often launch out, and,

as it were, lose themselves in His immensity, and, at times, several of these passions acting together in the soul, the noble disorder they cause cannot but affect the animal spirits, and communicate itself more or less to the body. Hence came the floods of tears shed by David, Jeremiah, Mary, Peter, Paul, etc. ; hence came the sighs, tears, strong cries, and groans unutterable of our Saviour Himself."

The " Defence," from which these extracts are made, fairly exhibits the mind of early Methodism, and of the Evangelical Revival generally, upon the questions discussed. The discrimination between religious feeling arising from the quickened apprehension of Divine truth, and that which is little more than natural emotion unnaturally stimulated, is not peculiar to Fletcher. He did but share it with the other leaders of the new reformation. The teaching of Wesley, the master mind of the whole movement, is, as regards this matter, as much marked by strong sense as by Evangelical fervour.

The comment, perhaps, of most readers of this " Defence of Experimental Religion " will be that the points contended for are obvious and indisputable, that they would be so readily admitted as to render much of the argument superfluous. That this should appear so is one of the many illustrations of the extent to which the results of the great Revival have passed into the religious life of the nation, and become a common heritage.

The private letters written at this period of Fletcher's life contain very little biographic material, and indeed

record few incidents of any kind.   Written, for the
most part, to persons like-minded with himself, they
consist mainly of the outpourings of praise and holy
aspiration, mingled with exhortations and counsels.   To
the spiritually-minded who may read them they will
continue to interpret and justify themselves, but it must
be admitted that they do not belong to the rare and
precious class of writings that rank among the permanent
treasures of the Christian Church.   The distinction
between that which is " for an age," and that which is
" for all time," is nowhere more marked than in religious
literature.   Fletcher's letters nourished the spiritual life
of his friends and correspondents, and were much read
by Methodists for a generation or two; but they have
failed to win a place among the books that do not grow
old, those companions of the spiritual life whose ministry
is from generation to generation.   So few indeed are the
books of this class that there is no need to apologise for
Fletcher because he has not added to their number.[1]

---

[1] The characteristic of Fletcher's letters which we consider their
greatest blemish is the frequent spiritualizing of common facts and
incidents.   We will illustrate our meaning.   His friend Mr. Ireland had sent him a hamper of wine, and some cloth to be made
into a suit of clothes.   In acknowledging the present, he says :
" Your broadcloth can lap me round two or three times ; but the
mantle of Divine love, the precious fine robe of Jesus's righteousness, can cover your soul a thousand times.   The cloth, fine and
good as it is, will not keep out a hard shower ; but that garment of
salvation will keep out even a shower of brimstone and fire.   Your
cloth will wear out ; but that fine linen, the righteousness of saints,
will appear with a finer lustre the more it is worn.   The moth may
fret your present, or the tailor may spoil it in cutting it ; but the

A few extracts from his correspondence may be given.

To the Rev. Charles Wesley.

"*Sept. 20th,* 1762.

"The 'crede quod habes et habes' is not very different from those words of Christ, 'What things soever ye desire, when ye pray, believe that ye receive them, and ye shall have them.' The humble reason of the believer and the irrational presumption of the enthusiast draw this doctrine to the right hand or to the left. But to split the hair, here lies the difficulty

---

present which Jesus has made you is out of reach of the spoiler, and ready for present wear." These comparisons are pursued consider-ably further, and then the other part of Mr. Ireland's present has its turn. "As I shall take a little of your wine for my stomach's sake, take you a good deal of the wine of the kingdom for your soul's sake. Every promise of the gospel is a bottle, a cask that has a spring within, and can never be exhausted. Draw the cork of unbelief, and drink abundantly. Be not afraid of intoxication; and if an inflammation follows, it will only be that of Divine love."

On another, but similar, occasion he writes to his good friend, "I want the living water rather than cider, and righteousness more than clothes."

These are not the extremest instances that Fletcher's letters afford of his habit of "spiritualising." It is plain that no suspicion of anything incongruous in his comparisons ever crossed his mind. Happy the man of whom it can be said that the only quality in which he is deficient is a sense of humour!

Wesley's remark upon this characteristic of Fletcher's style is: "This facility of raising useful observations from the most trifling incidents was one of those peculiarities in him which cannot be pro-posed to our imitation. . . . What was becoming and graceful in Mr. Fletcher would be disgustful almost in any other."

G

. . . Truly you are a pleasant casuist. What! 'It hath pleased Thee to regenerate this infant with Thy Holy Spirit, to receive him for Thine own child by adoption, and to incorporate him into Thy holy Church'—does all this signify nothing more than 'being taken into the visible Church'?

"How came you to think of my going to leave Madeley? I have indeed had my scruples about the above passage, and some in the burial service; but you may dismiss your fears, and be assured I will neither marry nor leave my Church without advising you."

To MISS HATTON.

"Nov. 1st, 1762.

"That there is a seal of pardon and an earnest of our inheritance above, to which you are as yet a stranger, seems clear from the tenor of your letter; but had I been in the place of the gentleman you name, I would have endeavoured to lay it before you as 'the fruit of faith,' and a most glorious privilege, rather than as 'the root of faith,' and a thing absolutely necessary to the being of it. . . . Hold fast your confidence, but do not trust nor rest in it; trust in Christ, and remember He says, 'I am the way'; not for you to stop, but to run on in Him. Rejoice to hear that there is a full assurance of faith to be obtained by the seal of God's Spirit, and go on from faith to faith until you are possessed of it. But remember this, and let this double advice prevent your straying to the right or left: first, that you will have reason to suspect the sincerity of your zeal if you lie down easy without the seal of your pardon, and the full assurance of your faith; secondly, while you wait for that seal in all the means of grace, beware of being unthankful for the least degree of faith and confidence in Jesus, beware of burying one talent, because you have not five, beware of despising the grain of mustard seed because it is not yet a tree.

"With respect to myself: in many conflicts and troubles of soul I have consulted many masters of the spiritual life; but Divine mercy did not, does not, suffer me to rest upon the word of a fellow creature. The best advices have often increased my perplexities; and the end was to make me cease from human dependence, and wait upon God from the dust of self-despair. To Him therefore I desire to point you and myself, in the person of Jesus Christ. This incarnate God receives weary, perplexed sinners still, and gives them solid rest. He teaches as no man ever taught; His words have spirit and life; nor can He possibly mistake our case."

Fletcher's correspondence with Miss Hatton continued, at intervals, for some years. She was much afflicted in body, and, as it would seem, harassed and burdened in spirit, and his letters afforded her consolation and guidance until the close of her life, to which he thus refers: "Poor Miss Hatton died last Sunday fortnight full of serenity, faith, and love. The four last hours of her life were better than all her sickness. When the pangs of death were upon her, the comforts of the Almighty bore her triumphantly through, and some of her last words were: "Grieve not at my happiness. . . . I wish I could tell you half of what I feel and see. I am going to keep an everlasting sabbath. . . . Thanks be to God, who giveth me the victory!"

His care for his people found expression in many ways that watchful love suggested, or their necessities seemed to call for. During his occasional absences from home he addressed pastoral letters to his flock filled with Christian exhortations and counsels. The following are extracts:

"*Oct.,* 1765.

"I beg you will not neglect the assembling of yourselves together, and when you meet in society, be neither backward nor forward to speak. Let every one esteem himself the meanest in the company, and be glad to sit at the feet of the lowest. . . . I had not time to finish this letter yesterday, being called upon to preach in a market town in the neighbourhood. . . . A gentleman churchwarden would hinder my getting into the pulpit, and, in order to do this, cursèd and swore, and took another gentleman by the collar in the middle of the church. Notwithstanding his rage, I preached. May the Lord raise in power what was sown in weakness!"

"*Sept.,* 1766.

"When I was in London I endeavoured to make the most of my time, that is to say, to hear, receive, and practise the word. Accordingly I went to Mr. Whitefield's tabernacle, and heard him give his society a most excellent exhortation upon love. He began by observing, that 'when St. John was old, and past walking and preaching, he would not forsake the assembling himself with the brethren, as the manner of too many is, upon little or no pretence at all. On the contrary, he got himself carried to their meeting, and, with his last thread of voice, preached to them his final sermon, consisting of this one sentence, "My little children, love one another."' I wish, I pray, I earnestly beseech you to follow that evangelical, apostolical advice. . . . Bear with one another's infirmities, and do not easily cast off any one; no, not for sin, except it be obstinately persisted in."

From unpublished manuscripts of Fletcher we find that in the latter part of the year 1764 he was engaged in a somewhat remarkable controversy within his own parish. His opponent was a Mrs. Anne Darby, a member of the Society of Friends, and the subjects discussed included the Athanasian Creed, the doctrine of the Trinity, the Sacraments, and the Christian Ministry. His account of its origin is as follows :

"On Thursday, November 22nd, 1764, Mrs. Darby, a female teacher among the people called Quakers, came into a house where the Vicar of Madeley was instructing his parishioners. He had given previous notice of his design to answer the objections made by dissenters and infidels against the Church of England; and he happened at her coming to defend the doctrine of the blessed Trinity, as contained in Athanasius's Creed.

" It was not long before the lady began the attack, and having given us a scriptural account of the Trinity, she blamed us for two things :

" 1st. For dwelling upon that point rather than enforcing practical duties.

" 2nd. For admitting St. Athanasius's Creed, as in her opinion it is full of gross misrepresentations of the Godhead."

A verbal discussion followed, which is carefully recorded. Mrs. Darby afterwards brought the six following questions, and put them to the vicar, who, in turn, furnishes a written reply.

" *1st Query*. Dost thou believe that thy Church, or as it is called, the Church of England, is the Church of Christ ?

" *2nd Query*. Dost thou believe that thou art a minister of Christ ?

" *3rd Query*. But Christ's ministers had all their trade. Was not Paul a tentmaker ? And is thy maintenance such as suits a minister of the gospel ?

" *4th Query*. The ministers of Christ preach the gospel freely. '*Freely ye have received, freely give,*' says Christ. Dost thou do so ?

" *5th Query*. Is the baptism thou baptizest with, the baptism of Him who baptized with the Holy Ghost ?

" *6th Query*. Dost thou believe that the supper thou celebratest is the supper of which Christ said, '*I stand at the door, and knock: if any man hear My voice, and open, I will come in, and sup with him, and he with Me*' ? "

In discussing these queries Fletcher took great pains.

He deals with no less than fifteen "objections" under one of them. Instead of asserting his authority, or that of the Church, he set himself to answer every reasonable question, including some that would hardly be considered such, to give satisfaction, if possible, to his opponents, and protect his people from what appeared to him serious perversions of truth. The labour involved would have sufficed to produce a book, but he had no literary aim in the matter. His manuscript was submitted to Mrs. Darby, and then, bound in a stout leathern cover, circulated among his parishioners. As we have quoted its opening passage, we will give an extract from its close, in which the Vicar of Madeley and Mrs. Darby take leave of one another.

"I hope the reader by this time laments with me the *bad* use that Mrs. Darby makes of a *good* understanding. How much better were it for her, and us all, if, instead of quibbling and wresting the Scriptures, as these sheets show she hath done, she would second the endeavours of the vicar in promoting a reformation of *essentials* in the parish with respect to principles and manners !

"But if she is still *moved by the spirit of contention* to make fresh assaults upon us, and to obtrude George Fox's peculiar tenets, to the disparagement of St. Paul's doctrines, we cannot but wish she may have a *better memory* to *remember* our answers, and *more candour* to do our arguments *justice*.

"In the meantime if the Vicar hath avoided the force of any of her objections, or omitted answering any, and if he has mistaken her in anything, he is ready to

acknowledge it, as soon as she hath made it appear;
and he hopes that if she acts by him as he hath assured
her by words of mouth he would do by her, she will
recall the copies of her partial manuscript, and correct
them, according to the mistakes I have pointed out
therein, before she makes them circulate any further."

To this is appended in Mrs. Darby's writing :

" Being called upon for this manuscript before I had
considered it all over properly, I therefore have got it
copied; and after examination (if worth notice) shall
communicate my sentiments hereupon to John Fletcher
and sober people.   A. Darby."

What further came of this controversy, whether anything further came of it, we cannot tell.   With Mrs.
Darby's postscript before us it would not be safe to
conclude that the last word had been spoken.

Among the labours belonging to this period was the
organization of a "Society of Ministers of the Gospel,"
for which Fletcher drew up rules and regulations.   Although, as we have seen, at the beginning of his work in
Madeley he had met with a good deal of opposition from
neighbouring clergy, he found it possible a few years
later to form a clerical association for the promotion
of spiritual life and ministerial efficiency.   The society
was to meet at Worcester, in the private house of some
reputable person, twice in the year, on the Tuesday
and Wednesday next before the full of the moon, in the
months of May and September.   The meeting was to
begin at ten o'clock, dinner at two; the expense to be
defrayed by an equal contribution of the whole society,

"*absentees not excepted.*" The topics for conversation and inquiry are set forth in considerable detail. They include "public preaching, the case of religious societies, the catechizing of children and instruction of youth, the case of personal inspection and personal visiting of the flock, the case of ruling their own houses well, the case of visiting the sick, the case of their own particular experiences and personal conduct."

Every member of the society was "recommended to take down brief minutes of the business transacted by the society, for his future recollection of it and meditation upon it."

The following are Fletcher's notes of the meeting held on May 12th, 1767 :

"1. How far is it proper to preach against particular sins, and to enforce particular duties, and how to do this in a gospel-like manner.

"*Answer.* Very proper to stated congregations. Many convinced of sin by it; many kept decent by it. Believers themselves made watchful. Preach so as not to encourage pharisees.

"2. Whether we are to preach the law, and morality, and why ?

"*Answer.* Yes: three reasons. (1) To inform believers; (2) To convince false moralists; (3) To stop the mouth of the adversaries, and confound antinomians.

"3. How far is it proper to mention and improve particular cases, and the experience of particular people, in funeral sermons and other discourses, to try to awaken the careless ?

"*Answer.* Extraordinary cases known to all may be improved—with tenderness, wisdom, avoiding the appearance of sentencing any one, and saying what we say of them in Scripture words, and with suppositions.

"4. (Digression.) Whether charity and duty oblige us to say over all the dead, 'we hope they rest in Christ.' (Settled.) (A hardship) and may be omitted because not insisted on as absolutely indispensable.

"6. What's the proper length of a sermon for hearers and speaker?

"*Answer.* A stranger may be heard for an hour; a stated minister from 30 to 50 minutes.

"7. What to do to keep within these bounds?

"*Answer.* Pray, digest the point, have few heads, be not long upon them. If you have been too full upon the first, be less so upon the last.

"8. When a minister hath studied a subject with design to preach on it, and is shut up in his heart and clouded in his mind at preaching time, and another text presents itself, and liberty is offered to speak from it, is it enthusiasm to do it?

"*Answer.* Trial may be made, and if the preacher finds freedom and the people edification, the matter was from above.

"9. Whether we may allegorize Scripture, and how far?

"*Answer.* So far as the Holy Ghost hath allegorized we may safely do the same; but we must be very sparing of anything that exceeds Scripture warrant. Avoid taking historical allegorical texts to raise doctrines upon. Such texts may be brought by way of comparison or illustration of some other weighty passages which contain the doctrine plainly.

" 10. Societies.

" *Disadvantages.* They raise a jealousy in those who 'do not belong to them, increase their prejudice, make them think the minister partial, and watch over the society for evil.

" *Advantages.* They are scriptural, comfortable, profitable, the only means of keeping up some discipline."

Such were the questions discussed, and the opinions expressed in the " Society of Ministers of the Gospel," organized, and probably founded, by Fletcher. The society was one of those innumerable results of the Revival, by which its spirit and principles were widely diffused through the Church. A generation later such associations were common amongst the Evangelical clergy. Of these the Eclectic Society, founded by John Newton and Richard Cecil in 1783, is well-known to us through the " Notes," extending from 1798 to 1814, published by Archdeacon Pratt.[1]

At the close of his first seven years at Madeley, Fletcher's chief difficulties had either disappeared, or were greatly diminished. Though he still lamented the

---

[1] In Archdeacon Pratt's " Eclectic Notes," pp. 185–189, there is an interesting discussion of one of the questions referred to above, viz. the advantages and disadvantages of religious societies. Mr. Venn is quoted as saying, " Dr. Woodward's societies were the first we read of. They might have existed to this day, had not Mr. Wesley's arisen."

comparative unfruitfulness of his labours, he had, in truth, much to rejoice over. Many of the ungodly had been converted through his ministry, some of whom were now walking worthy of Christ, while others had died in the Lord. He was now generally esteemed, and by the better part of his flock greatly beloved. He had gained experience in the administration of his parish and the direction of souls. In preaching, catechizing, visiting, and holding religious meetings he was indefatigable, and spared no pains to guard his people from doctrinal error or spiritual decline. The organization that gradually rose under his hand was not of the modern parochial type, but well suited to the circumstances of the people and of the time. He established regular preaching-places, not only in his own parish, but eight, ten, or more miles away, and formed societies for Christian instruction and fellowship. From time to time his hands were strengthened and his heart encouraged by visits from his friends and fellow labourers. Wesley's first visit was in July, 1764, and is thus referred to in his " Journal ":

"I rode to Bilbrook, near Wolverhampton, and preached at between two and three. Thence we went on to Madeley, an exceedingly pleasant village, encompassed with trees and hills. It was a great comfort to me to converse once more with a Methodist of the old type, denying himself, taking up his cross, and resolved to be altogether a Christian.

"*Sunday, July* 22*nd.* At ten Mr. Fletcher read prayers, and I preached on those words in the gospel,

'I am the Good Shepherd: the Good Shepherd layeth down His life for the sheep.' The church would nothing near contain the congregation; but a window near the pulpit being taken down, those who could not come in stood in the churchyard, and I believe all could hear. The congregation, they said, used to be much smaller in the afternoon than in the morning; but I could not discern the least difference, either in number or seriousness. I found employment enough for the intermediate hours in praying with the various companies who hung about the house, insatiably hungering and thirsting after the good word. Mr. Grimshaw, at his first coming to Haworth, had not such a prospect as this. There are many adversaries indeed, but yet they cannot shut the open and effectual door."

Wesley's itinerant preachers were welcomed by Fletcher when their rounds brought them to his parish. To Alexander Mather, a brave and devoted Methodist preacher, he wrote to say that an occasional exhortation from him or his colleague to the societies he had formed would be esteemed a favour, and expressed at the same time a willingness, if it were not deemed an encroachment, to go, as Providence might direct, to any of Mr. Mather's preaching-places.

And as Fletcher rejoiced in the evangelistic labours of others in his own neighbourhood, so he willingly engaged in similar labours himself in various parts of the country. In the year 1765 we find him exchanging pulpits for a while with Mr. Sellon, curate of Breedon, in Leicestershire, and preaching to the crowds who filled the church, and clambered to the windows to see and hear.

Two years later, having secured the services of an acceptable curate to serve the parish in his absence, he spent some weeks in Yorkshire with the Countess of Huntingdon and Mr. Venn, the Vicar of Huddersfield. They were joined by a number of earnest clergy from different parts of the country, Mr. Madan from London, Dr. Conyers, Rector of Helmsley, Mr. Burnet, Vicar of Elland, and several others, by whom the gospel was preached to multitudes in town and country. In such companionship and in such labours Fletcher rejoiced greatly, and returned to his parish with renewed strength. The sense of loneliness was relieved. The difficulties of his work at Madeley seemed no longer exceptional. Cheered by the success vouchsafed to his labours and those of his friends, he came back to his people "in the fulness of the blessing of Christ." Modern experience has shown how a parish or a congregation may be benefited by the coming of a mission preacher, and how a minister may be enlarged in heart and utterance by special labours away from his own flock. Missions based upon the recognition of these truths are now familiar to us all; but in this matter, as in so much of the quickened life of the Church, the men of the Revival led the way.

CHAPTER VIII.

TREVECCA COLLEGE.—THE CALVINIST CONTROVERSY.

IN the summer of 1768 Fletcher undertook an office which greatly increased his labours and responsibilities. The religious movement directed by the Countess of Huntingdon continuing to develop, a considerable number of chapels had, by this time, been built or hired in various parts of the country. The pulpits were generally supplied by clergymen of the Established Church, procured by the countess's personal influence. But such arrangements became increasingly difficult to make. Their 'irregularity' was disapproved in high quarters. Lady Huntingdon's chaplains were, in fact, as 'irregular' in their labours as Wesley's itinerant preachers. The system that found no place for the one could not long sanction the other; whilst her ladyship's ecclesiastical authority was a still greater anomaly than that of Wesley.

It became necessary therefore to meet the demand for earnest, evangelical preachers in some other way than by the services of the regular clergy. Meanwhile, the expulsion of six students from the University of Oxford for "being attached to the sect called Methodists, and holding their doctrines," showed that the university was hardly likely to be the nursing mother of such men as were required.

In these circumstances the countess resolved to found a school or college for the training of godly young men for the work of the ministry. She proposed to admit such as were truly converted to God and gave evidence of being called to preach the gospel, and to give them the advantage of three years' residence and instruction, at the close of which they might enter the ministry, either in the Church of England, or among Protestants of any other denomination. After taking counsel with Whitefield, Romaine, Venn, Fletcher, and others, Lady Huntingdon established the institution on which her heart was set.

Fletcher appears to have been in thorough sympathy with the countess's aims from the first. Being consulted as to the selection of books for the college, he writes : "Having studied abroad, and used rather foreign than English books with my pupils, I am not acquainted with the books Great Britain affords well enough to select the best and most concise. Besides, a plan of studies must be fixed upon first, before proper books can be chosen. Grammar, logic, rhetoric, with ecclesiastical history, and a little natural philosophy, and geography, with a great deal of practical divinity, will be enough for those who do not care to dive into languages. Mr. Townsend and Charles Wesley might, by spending an hour together, make a proper choice ; and I would recommend them not to forget Watts's ' Logic,' and his

' History of the Bible by Questions and Answers,' which seem to me excellent books of the kind for clearness and order. Mr. Wesley's 'Natural Philosophy' contains as much as is wanted, or more. Mason's 'Essay on Pronunciation' will be worth their attention. Henry and Gill on the Bible, with four volumes of Baxter's 'Practical Works,' Keach's 'Metaphors,' Taylor on the Types, Gurnal's 'Christian Armour,' Edwards on Preaching, Johnson's English dictionary, and Mr. Wesley's Christian Library, may make part of the little library. The book of Baxter I mention I shall take care to send to Trevecca, as a mite towards the collection, together with Usher's 'Body of Divinity,' Scapula's Greek lexicon, and Lyttleton's Latin dictionary."

But while Lady Huntingdon received counsel and assistance from many quarters, and from Fletcher amongst the rest, there was one service for which she looked to him alone. Would Fletcher allow himself to be placed at the head of her college? Would he accept the presidency, visiting Trevecca as often as he conveniently could, to direct the studies and discipline of the place, and test the character and qualifications of the students? From his profound esteem for the countess, and in the hope of assisting in the good work of raising up an earnest ministry, Fletcher accepted the office, and, without fee or reward of any kind, threw himself heartily into its duties.

An old mansion, known as Trevecca House, in the parish of Talgarth, South Wales, was altered and adapted to the requirements of a college ; tutors were procured,

H

and the house was soon filled with students, the first of whom was a young man from Madeley, converted under Fletcher's ministry. Lady Huntingdon herself took up her residence there, and by her presence stimulated the zeal of the household. Much of the time of the students was employed in evangelistic work. On foot or on horseback they visited the towns and villages for twenty or thirty miles round, preaching in chapels and houses, in field and market-places, as opportunity allowed. The pious founder soon saw a revival and extension of the work of God which filled her heart with joy, and assured her that the undertaking, concerning which some of her best friends had their misgivings, was approved by God. At the dedication of the college and chapel, on August 24th, 1768, Lady Huntingdon's birthday, Whitefield was the preacher, and large numbers of people came together from all parts of the country. The following year, the anniversary was the occasion of a still more remarkable gathering, and of a series of religious services marked by great manifestations of spiritual power. The most eminent ministers that Lady Huntingdon's summons could assemble were present. The congregations, too large for the chapel, assembled in the court. Day by day, and almost all day long, for a week together, vast crowds were moved to tears, to rapture, and to awe under the preaching of the gospel. Howel Harris, Howel Davies, and Daniel Rowlands, men whose names are household words in Wales to-day, preached in Welsh ; and Wesley, Fletcher, and Shirley in English. Thousands of voices rose in hymns of praise, and joined in fervent responses and cries of prayer. On the Saturday and Sunday, and again on the following Thursday, the Lord's supper was administered, and Fletcher addressed the communicants with an earnestness and pathos that it seemed impossible to withstand. Many were awakened and converted. "Truly God was in the midst of us," said Lady Huntingdon, "and many felt Him eminently nigh. The gracious influences of His Spirit seemed to rest on every soul. . . . Words fail to describe the holy triumph with which the great congregation sang—

'Captain of Thine enlisted host,
Display Thy glorious banner high.'"

After a week of never to be forgotten blessings, the great crowds slowly dispersed, and the tireless evangelists took horse and rode away, each to his work, with strength renewed, and spirit refreshed as from the presence of the Lord.

Although Fletcher did not reside at the college, his connexion with it was by no means a nominal one. His journeys to Trevecca were frequent, involving fatigue and privations, which his feeble frame could ill endure, though he counted them less than nothing. As to the character of his visits, and the influence that accompanied him, the testimony of Mr. Benson, the headmaster, himself a man of exceptional intelligence and sanctity, is well known, but is too important to be omitted here:

"Mr. Fletcher visited them frequently, and was received as an angel of God. It is not possible for me to describe the veneration in which we all held him. Like Elijah in the schools of the prophets, he was revered, he was loved, he was almost adored; and that, not only by every student, but by every member of the family. And indeed he was worthy. The reader will pardon me if he think I exceed. My heart kindles while I write. Here it was that I saw, shall I say an angel in human flesh? I should not far exceed the truth if I said so. But here I saw a descendant of fallen Adam so fully raised above the ruins of the fall, that though by the body he was tied down to earth, yet was his whole conversation in heaven, yet was his life, from day to day, hid with Christ in God. Prayer, praise, love, and zeal, all ardent, elevated above what one would think attainable in this state of frailty, were the element in which he continually lived. And as to others, his one employment was to call, entreat, and urge them to ascend with him to the glorious Source of being and blessedness. He had leisure comparatively for nothing else. Languages, arts, sciences, grammar, rhetoric, logic, even divinity itself, as it, is called, were all laid aside when he appeared in the schoolroom among the students. His full heart would not suffer him to be silent. He must speak, and they were readier to hearken to this servant and minister of Jesus Christ than to attend to Sallust, Virgil, Cicero, or any Latin or Greek historian, poet, or philosopher, they had been engaged in reading. And they seldom hearkened long before they were all in tears, and every heart catched fire from the flame which burned in his soul.

"These seasons generally terminated in this. Being convinced that to be filled with the Holy Ghost was a better qualification for the ministry of the gospel than any classical learning (although that too be useful in its place), after speaking awhile in the schoolroom, he used frequently to say, 'As many of you as are athirst for this fulness of the Spirit, follow me into my room.' On this many of us have instantly followed him, and there continued for two or three hours, wrestling like Jacob for the blessing, praying one after another, till we could bear to kneel no longer.

*　　*　　*　　*　　*

"Such was the ordinary employment of this man of God while he remained at Trevecca. He preached the word of life to the students and family, and as many of the neighbours as desired to be present. He was 'instant in season, and out of season'; he 'reproved, rebuked, exhorted, with all longsuffering.' He was always employed, either in illustrating some important truth, or exhorting to some neglected duty, or administering some needful comfort, or relating some useful anecdote, or making some profitable remark or observation upon some occurrence. And his devout soul, always burning with love and zeal, led him to intermingle prayer with all he uttered. Meanwhile his manner was so solemn, and at the same time so mild and insinuating, that it was hardly possible for any one who had the happiness of being in his company not to be struck with awe and charmed with love, as if in the presence of an angel or departed spirit. Indeed,

I frequently thought, while attending to his heavenly
discourse and Divine spirit, that he was so different
from, and superior to, the generality of mankind, as to
look more like Moses or Elijah, or some prophet or
apostle, come again from the dead, than a mortal man, ·
dwelling in a house of clay. It is true, his weak and
long-afflicted body proclaimed him to be human ; but
the graces which so eminently filled and adorned his soul
manifested him to be Divine : and long before his happy
spirit returned to God who gave it, that which was
human seemed in a great measure to be 'swallowed up
of life.'"

Benson was not alone in the impressions he received
of Fletcher's character, and of the influence he exercised
at Trevecca.   The references of others are in the same
strain ; and although his connexion with the college
came to an abrupt end, and was followed by a period
of painful controversy, we hear no disparagement of his
piety, or suggestion of anything unworthy of his reputation for Christian meekness and purity.

But why did Fletcher so soon withdraw from the
presidency of the college?   To use the words of Mr.
Benson : " Why did he give up an office for which he
was perfectly well qualified, which he executed so
entirely to the satisfaction of all the parties concerned,
and in which it pleased God to give so manifest a
blessing to his labours ?"   The answer is, that it was
one of the first results of a controversy which, for
intensity, for duration, and for the strifes and divisions
to which it gave rise, is unhappily memorable in the

history of the Revival. Its very name—the Calvinistic controversy—will suggest to the experienced reader the range of questions involved, and the improbability of agreement being arrived at, however prolonged might be the discussion.

It should be borne in mind that, from its very beginning, the Revival had advanced along two different lines, in connexion with certain well-marked doctrinal distinctions. Whilst the work and the workers in the two spheres were, in the best and deepest sense, one, they were divided upon those questions concerning predestination and free will, which, since the time of Augustine, have given rise to two distinct types of doctrine, each susceptible of modifications and developments of its own. This difference was represented, first in the little band of Oxford Methodists, and then in the more evangelical and expansive Methodism that succeeded it. Wesley was an Arminian, and Whitefield a Calvinist. Harmonious co-operation between them was at times difficult; but mutual love and largeness of heart prevailed upon the whole.

Under Wesley's leadership, Arminian Methodism developed in organic form, and is still found in all parts of the world in visible, organized Churches. Calvinistic Methodism spread with similar, if not equal, rapidity, but without unity of administration, and failed to develop any principles of Church life. It revived the Calvinistic nonconformity of England, and may almost be said to have taken possession of Wales; but the main current of its strength flowed into the Church

of England, and is to be traced in the rise and progress
of the Evangelical or Low Church party. There may
be difference of opinion as to which development has
been on the whole of greater service to the Christian
Church, but few persons will deny to either a high place
in the order of Providence.

At the period we have now reached in Fletcher's
history, a certain uneasiness may be discovered in the
relations of Arminian and Calvinistic Methodism, not
incompatible however with such union and brotherli-
ness as were seen at the great gathering at Trevecca.
But Wesley was observing with concern the spread of
a practical antinomianism, which on every possible
ground he hated and feared. The openly wicked were
hopeful and comparatively harmless compared with
persons who talked fluently of being justified and
sanctified, while they were guilty of drunkenness, un-
cleanness, and dishonesty. This state of things he
could not and would not endure, if it was to be prevented
by plainness of doctrine or rigour of discipline. He
knew that while such abuses were not the necessary
accompaniment of the Scriptural doctrine of faith, they
arose from a perversion to which that doctrine will
always be exposed, and against which it will be needful
to guard, as long as human nature is what it is. Any
language therefore that tended to weaken the sense of
moral responsibility, or lower the standard of Christian
duty, was doubly dangerous in presence of a tendency
to dwell upon the Divine sovereignty in redemption, to
the neglect of the Divine requirements, as they are

revealed to man in the gospel. In Wesley's judgment, his preachers were in danger of encouraging, or at least giving opportunity to, antinomian error by using expressions that had received a kind of general sanction, and refraining from certain others which were thought too legal and unevangelic. But what had this to do with Calvinism? Some writers, more jealous for the character of Wesley's societies than he was, will have it that the abuses referred to were mainly or entirely to be found amongst the Calvinists. But that is not the case. As Mr. Watson has well said : " To show however that antinomianism can graft itself upon other stocks besides that of the Calvinistic decrees, it was found also among the Moravians, and the Methodists did not escape. . . . In fact, there is no such exclusive connexion between the more sober Calvinistic theories of predestination and this great error, as some have supposed." With this statement Wesley would, we think, have agreed ; but he undoubtedly held that antinomianism was a much more natural and likely result of Calvinistic than of Arminian principles.

In the one case the principles must be violated, in the other they had only to be developed and applied to produce the evils referred to. Moreover. Calvinism, as popularly understood, had lost what safeguards it possessed, and had little in common with that of Owen, and Leighton, and Matthew Henry. Spiritual pride and carnal indulgence flourished along with a crude and coarse belief in unconditional election and imputed righteousness. With Calvinism in its purely theological

and philosophical aspects Wesley felt no call to deal.
It was wholly a practical question with him. He saw,
or thought he saw, that its principles were doing actual
mischief, and that, amongst other things, the every-day
language of religion was being corrupted by phrases and
catchwords that encouraged serious error. A quarter of
a century ago, at the first Methodist Conference, the
question was asked, " Have we not unawares leaned
too much to Calvinism ? *Answer :* We are afraid we
have." Might it not be time to ask this question again,
and answer it in a less uncertain manner ? Wesley
judged it was. Accordingly, the " Minutes of Conference " for 1770 contain the following statement :

"We said, in 1744, 'We have leaned too much
toward Calvinism.' Wherein ?

" 1. With regard to *man's faithfulness.* Our Lord
Himself taught us to use the expression. And we
ought never to be ashamed of it. We ought steadily
to assert, on His authority, that if a man is not 'faithful
in the unrighteous mammon,' God will not give him
' *the true riches.'*

" 2. With regard to *working for life.* This also our
Lord has expressly commanded us. ' Labour (ἐργάζεσθε,
literally, 'work') for the meat that endureth to everlasting
life.' And, in fact, every believer, till he comes to glory,
works *for* as well as *from* life.

" 3. We have received it as a maxim that 'a man is
to do nothing in order to justification.' Nothing can be
more false. Whoever desires to find favour with God,
should ' cease from evil, and learn to do well.' Who-

ever repents should do 'works meet for repentance.' And if this is not *in order* to find favour, what does he do them for?

"Review the whole affair.

"1. Who of us is *now* accepted of God?

"He that now believes in Christ, with a loving and obedient heart.

"2. But who among those that never heard of Christ?

"He that feareth God, and worketh righteousness, according to the light he has.

"3. Is this the same with 'he that is sincere'?

"Nearly, if not quite.

"4. Is not this 'salvation by works'?

"Not by the *merit* of works, but by works as a *condition.*

"5. What have we then been disputing about for these thirty years?

"I am afraid, *about words.*

"6. As to *merit* itself, of which we have been so dreadfully afraid: we are rewarded 'according to our works,' yea, 'because of our works.' How does this differ from *for the sake of our works?* And how differs this from *secundum merita operum?* As our works *deserve.*

"Can you split this hair?

"I doubt I cannot." *

---

* More than half a century afterwards, when all the parties to this controversy had passed away, and time had given opportunity for a calm estimate of the whole matter, Mr. Watson, at once the most competent and the most reverential of Wesley's biographers, expressed himself as follows, concerning the "Minutes" of 1770 :

The reader, who has, it may be, glanced rapidly over the preceding paragraphs, without perceiving in them anything very portentous, will be surprised to learn that their publication gave rise to the longest and sharpest controversy in the history of Methodism. An ancient controversy has this in common with an extinct volcano, that after generations may walk all unconscious over the cold ashes of what was once a glowing lava torrent. To Wesley's contemporaries these " Minutes " were full of meaning ; every allusion was recognised, every phrase touched some active belief or disbelief. Amongst the Calvinists generally, and more particularly in Lady Huntingdon's circle, they caused the utmost indignation and alarm. Wesley was denounced as a heretic, an apostate, a papist unmasked. Lady Huntingdon wept over them, called them "horrible and abominable," and declared that "whosoever did not fully, and without any evasion, disavow them should not stay in her college."

" That there were passages calculated to awaken suspicion, and that they gave the appearance of inconsistency to Mr. Wesley's opinions, and indicated a tendency to run to one extreme in order to avoid another—an error which Mr. Wesley more generally avoided than most men,—cannot be denied. . . .

" Mr. Wesley acknowledged that the 'minutes' were 'not sufficiently guarded.' This must be felt by all; they were out of his usual manner of expressing himself, and he had said the same truths often, in a clearer, and safer, and even stronger manner. He certainly did not mean to alter his previous opinions, or formally to adopt other terms in which to express them, and therefore to employ new modes of speaking, though for a temporary purpose, was not without danger, although they were capable of an innocent explanation."

Lady Glenorchy "must bear her feeble testimony against the sentiments contained in them. . . . She has always countenanced Mr. Wesley's preachers, but now she finds this cannot be done by her any longer." Mr. Shirley pronounced them "dreadful heresy," "injurious to the very fundamental principles of Christianity," and said publicly that he deemed "peace in such a case a shameful indolence, and silence no less than treachery." Active measures were taken for the vindication of outraged orthodoxy. Every Arminian must quit the college. Mr. Benson, the headmaster, declined to disavow the sentiments of the "Minutes," and was consequently dismissed. Fletcher felt compelled to write: "Mr. Benson made a very just defence when he said he held with me the possibility of salvation for all men; that mercy is offered to all, and yet may be received or rejected. If this be what your ladyship calls Mr. Wesley's opinion, free-will, and Arminianism, and if 'every Arminian must quit the college,' I am actually discharged also." In the hope of mediating between Wesley and the countess, Fletcher went to Trevecca. He tried to soften matters, but in vain. He then absolutely resigned his office, advised Lady Huntingdon to choose a moderate Calvinist in his place, and recommended Rowland Hill. His letter to Wesley (first published by Mr. Tyerman*), giving an account of his interview with Lady Huntingdon, and beseeching his venerated friend to believe "that the college and its

---

* "Wesley's Designated Successor," pp. 177–179.

foundress mean well, and give them all the satisfaction
you can," is in his finest vein of good sense, elevated
and illumined by Christian feeling.

But, unhappily, no private and friendly understanding
was arrived at. As the time for Wesley's next Conference drew near, a circular letter, signed "Walter
Shirley," was sent round among the friends of the
Evangelical movement, proposing that those who disapproved the obnoxious minutes "should go in a body to
the said Conference, and insist upon a formal recan-
tation of the said minutes, and in case of a refusal sign
and publish their protest against them." This proposed
demonstration however, from various causes, dwindled
down to a small deputation, which presented itself,
meekly enough, at the Conference at Bristol, and was
received by Wesley and the preachers in a friendly
manner. The spirit of conciliation was in the ascendant.
Wesley and all his preachers present, except one, signed
a declaration admitting that the minutes were not sufficiently guarded in the way they were expressed, and
repudiating the meaning which had been put upon
them, viz. that of justification by works. Mr. Shirley,
in return, wrote a memorandum to the effect that "the
declaration agreed to in Conference, August 8th, 1771,
had convinced him that he had mistaken the meaning
of the doctrinal points in the 'Minutes of the Conference,
held in London, August 7th, 1770'; and he hereby wished
to testify the full satisfaction he had in the said declaration, and his hearty concurrence and agreement with the
same."

Why did not the matter end here? Might not such explanations and concessions have secured peace? Was a seven years war absolutely necessary? To this question we have met with no really satisfactory reply. But it must now be mentioned that, prior to the assembling of the Conference at Bristol, Fletcher had written a "Vindication" of the much discussed minutes in the form of "Five Letters" to Mr. Shirley. The manuscript of this "Vindication" was in Wesley's hands, and was, in fact, being set up in type at the very time that Shirley and his friends were having their interview with Wesley and the Conference. The question is, whether the publication should have been proceeded with in the turn that things had taken. Shirley, hearing that Fletcher's "Letters" were in the press, not unnaturally requested that the issue might be stopped. Fletcher himself wrote to his friend Mr. Ireland: "I feel for poor dear Mr. Shirley, whom I have (considering the present circumstances) treated too severely in my 'Vindication of the Minutes.' My dear sir, what must be done? I am ready to defray, by selling to my last shirt, the expense of the printing of my 'Vindication,' and suppress it. Direct me, dear sir. Consult with Mr. Shirley and Mr. Wesley about the matter. Be persuaded I am ready to do everything that will be brotherly in this unhappy affair." But in Wesley's judgment nothing that had taken place required the suppression of so admirable a "tract for the times," and accordingly it was published. Opinions will be divided as to the wisdom and propriety of the step. It may be said : " The merely personal aspect of the question was now disposed of. But the evils which had led to the recording of the 'minutes' were real evils, and were not to be got rid of by an interchange of courtesies between Wesley and the Conference on the one hand, and Lady Huntingdon and Mr. Shirley on the other. Circumstances, or rather Providence, had discovered—nay, raised up—in Fletcher the very man for the present need. What could be better, in the interest of true religion, than to send forth broadcast, not merely a 'Vindication of the Minutes,' and of Wesley's action, but a powerful defence of the gospel itself against the chief and most dangerous error of the day?" There could be no mistake as to the value of what Fletcher had written. His argument was clear in outline, and convincing in detail. The gospel way of salvation was defended on the right hand and on the left. Popular errors were exposed, paradoxes explained, and misunderstanding removed, with a knowledge of the Scriptures and a skill in reasoning that astonished every one. The meek Vicar of Madeley was a master of controversy. He had learning and logic for scholars, with imagination, wit, and pathos to charm the common people. The style was genial and easy, abounding in lively comparisons and illustrations, while a gentle vein of humour, stopping short of bitterness on the one hand, and burlesque on the other, mingled, not unbecomingly, with passages of the most exalted devotion. " Those letters," wrote Wesley, " could not be suppressed, without betraying the honour of our Lord." This decided his action.

Of course Fletcher's letters had their reply from Mr. Shirley, and that, in turn, required to be answered. Then Richard Hill entered the field, and him also Fletcher encountered, and as the controversy grew it spread out over the wide area of questions speculative and practical which the term Calvinism covers or suggests, and called fresh combatants into the field. We have no heart to pursue the details of this history. It is complicated and unremunerative in the last degree. It deepened into bitterness and scurrility, till its baser literature becomes unreadable for very shame; it separated brethren; it turned allies into adversaries; it offered to a sceptical and ungodly age the spectacle of good men " smiting one another *un*friendly," and consumed time and strength that were wanted, and more than wanted, for the Christianising of the country.

Through all this strife and confusion we can at least follow Fletcher without shame, if not without regret. We have already quoted Southey's eulogy on him. It is not excessive. He kept his temper through seven years of trying controversy. He lived and wrote " as ever in his great Taskmaster's eye." Love to God is manifest in every page, and only second to it is love for those with whom he must needs contend, a veritable " longing after them in the bowels of Jesus Christ."

Fletcher's " Checks " were the best thing born of the controversy. They did not,—need it be said ?—finally dispose of the problems respecting God's foreknowledge and sovereignty, and the free agency and responsibility of man. These problems are perhaps much where

I

they were when first confronted. If they are less discussed in our own day than formerly, it is not that the
difficulties they present have been solved, but that a
juster estimate of the limits of our powers, together with
a deeper sense of the antinomies of Divine law, has in a
great measure withdrawn the Christian mind from these
questions to more remunerative ones. That the doctrines commonly· called Calvinistic logically lead either
to presumption or despair, may perhaps fairly be urged ;
that they do so as matter of fact, and on any wide scale,
would be difficult to prove. But whether the vulgar
antinomianism of Fletcher's day had or had not its roots
in Calvinistic doctrine, his handling of it as a practical
matter is vigorous and effective in the highest degree.
He pursues it in all its forms. He exposes and refutes
those one-sided reasonings which " make for *un*righteousness"; he sets forth law in gospel, and gospel in
law, with admirable balance and proportion; he exhibits
Christian holiness as the sum of duty and the crown
of privilege, and breathes throughout a heavenly spirit,
which the warmth of controversy seldom, if ever, disturbs.

May we say then, as some one has said, "it was
worth while to have the Calvinistic controversy, if it
were only for the sake of Fletcher's contribution to it"?
Our answer is, most emphatically, No. We have too
deep a sense of the evils of a long and embittered strife
between good men to pass any such judgment. Nor
can we suppose that such a controversy furnished the
only, or even the most favourable, conditions for the

exercise of Fletcher's gifts. We should have preferred for him—can we doubt that he would have preferred for himself?—the opportunity of writing books "touching the King" without the necessity for splitting hairs with Shirley, and for winnowing the coarse abuse of Toplady, and the extravagances of Rowland and Richard Hill.

But while we regard the controversy as both an error and an evil, we are far from denying that it had its compensations, for which we are indebted almost exclusively to Fletcher. His writings undoubtedly served to fasten deep discredit upon that imperfect gospel—"another gospel, which is not another,"—which permits its followers "to continue in sin that grace may abound." Without lowering or lessening the doctrine of justification by faith, Fletcher gave new emphasis and clearer setting to the doctrine of Christian holiness, and rescued Christian ethics from disparagement and neglect. Without taking away from the virtue of the atonement in its relation to the whole standing of the believer, he enforced that great practical end of redemption, "the righteousness of the law, fulfilled in men walking not after the flesh, but after the Spirit." Towards the close of the year 1774 Wesley wrote, "If we could once bring all our preachers, itinerant and local, uniformly and steadily to insist on those two points, 'Christ dying for us,' and 'Christ reigning in us,' we should shake the trembling gates of hell. I think most of them are now exceeding clear herein, and the rest come nearer, especially since they have read Mr. Fletcher's

' Checks,' which have removed many difficulties out of the way."

Fletcher's " Checks to Antinomianism " at once took a foremost place in the literature of Methodism. Wesley recommended them to his followers with all the weight of his authority. The interest awakened by the controversy, the popular style in which they were written, and the elevation and fervour of piety manifest throughout, carried them into every Methodist household. They were studied by the preachers, and read for spiritual edification by all the more earnest members of the Society. They did much to nourish the spiritual life of such men and women as Bramwell, and Carvosso, and Hester Ann Rogers, names that adorn and interpret the Methodist doctrine of " Entire Sanctification." It is not too much to say that for many years they were not least among the instruments employed in connexion with the ever-extending Revival, " for the perfecting of the saints, . . . for the edifying of the body of Christ."

In more recent times the influence of this, Fletcher's principal work, is indirect rather than direct. It fills the atmosphere of the Methodist Churches with a kind of after-glow. Its light and heat linger in the air, and are reflected from the regions where its first full strength was felt. Should these writings come, in course of time, to be entirely neglected, that influence would still be felt, for it has passed beyond recall into the theology and devotional literature of Methodism all the world over. Two of the most competent historians of Methodism, Dr. Stevens and Mr. Tyerman, give it as their opinion that Fletcher's "Checks" are as much read to-day as they were a hundred years ago. From this opinion we are constrained to dissent, and should be content to refer the matter to the Methodist publishing houses for decision. We believe, on the contrary, that they are very little read ; but none the less are we persuaded that the results of Fletcher's controversial labours are, in many respects, permanent ; and, in addition to those ·that have been referred to, we would instance the fact that Calvinistic doctrine has come to be better guarded against the perversions of antinomianism, and that disputes arising out of it have become less frequent and more moderate, to the great advantage of the Christian Church.

In passing from this subject we cannot refrain from quoting a few paragraphs from his "First Check," in which Fletcher reveals his love and reverence for Wesley :

"A gray-headed minister of Christ, an old general in the armies of Emmanuel, a father who has children capable of instructing even masters in Israel ; and. one whom God made the first and principal instrument of the late Revival of internal religion in our Church. . . . One word more about Mr. Wesley, and I have done. Of the two greatest and most useful ministers I ever knew, one is no more. The other, after amazing labours, flies still with unwearied diligence through the three kingdoms, calling sinners to repentance, and to the healing fountain of Jesus' blood. Though oppressed with the weight of near seventy years and the care of near 30,000 souls, he shames still, by his unabated zeal and immense labours, all the young ministers in England, perhaps in Christendom. He has generally blown the gospel trump, and rode twenty miles, before most of the professors who despise his labours have left their downy pillow. As he begins the day, the week, the year, so he concludes them, still intent upon extensive services for the glory of the Redeemer and the good of souls. And shall we lightly lift up our pens, our tongues, our hands against him? No; let them rather forget their cunning! If we *will* quarrel, can we find nobody to fall out with, but the minister upon whom God puts the greatest honour?

"Our Elijah has lately been translated to heaven.[1] Gray-headed Elisha is yet awhile continued upon earth. And shall we make a hurry and noise, to bring in railing accusations against him with more success? . . . Shall the sons of the prophets, shall even children in grace and knowledge, openly traduce the venerable seer, and his abundant labours?"

This description of Wesley may serve to introduce an incident showing Wesley's opinion of Fletcher.

---

[1] Referring to the death of Whitefield in 1770.

CHAPTER IX

WESLEY'S PROPOSAL.—FAILING HEALTH.

WESLEY'S estimate of Fletcher's character and abilities had been, from the first, uniformly high, but the circumstances connected with the Calvinist controversy raised it still higher. Every one knew of Fletcher's gentleness and simplicity, but no one was prepared for the strength, the firmness, the mental vigour and versatility that he now exhibited. If this was something of a surprise to Wesley, it was matter of unfeigned rejoicing. He saw, or thought he saw, in Fletcher a man fitted for a greater work than that of being Vicar of Madeley. It was natural perhaps that Wesley should never quite appreciate the position of a parochial minister. His belief in itinerancy had its roots in his temperament, as well as in his judgment. He said of himself, that if he were confined to one spot, he should preach himself and his whole congregation to sleep in a twelvemonth. He always grudged Fletcher to his obscure parish, and the feeling grew with every fresh manifestation of Fletcher's powers. The conviction began to take shape in his mind that Fletcher was the proper man to succeed him in the direction of the Methodist preachers and societies. He was now nearly seventy years of age, and his health was apparently failing. In the course of things he must shortly lay down his work. Who was there to take it up? It could not be that God would suffer it to fall to pieces for want of one to control and guide it; and who was there that could compare in fitness with Fletcher? Wesley determined therefore not to leave this matter to the last, but to communicate with him while there was yet time. Accordingly, in January, 1773, he wrote to him as follows :

" Dear Sir,—

What an amazing work has God wrought in these kingdoms in less than forty years! And it not only continues, but increases, throughout England, Scotland, and Ireland ; nay, it has lately spread into New York, Pennsylvania, Virginia, Maryland, and Carolina. But the wise men oŧ the world say, 'When Mr. Wesley drops, then all this is at an end!' And so it surely will, unless, before God calls him hence, one is found to stand in his place. I see more and more, unless there be one προεστώς, the work can never be carried on. The body of the preachers are not united, nor will any part of them submit to the rest; so that either there must be one to preside over all, or the work will indeed come to an end.

"But who is sufficient for these things? qualified to preside both over the preachers and people? He must be a man of faith and love, and one that has

a single eye to the advancement of the kingdom of
God. He must have a clear understanding; a knowledge of men and things, particularly of the Methodist
doctrine and discipline; a ready utterance; diligence
and activity, with a tolerable share of health. There
must be added to these favour with the people, with
the Methodists in general; for, unless God turn their
eyes and their hearts towards him, he will be quite
incapable of the work. He must likewise have some
degree of learning, because there are many adversaries, learned as well as unlearned, whose mouths must
be stopped. But this cannot be done unless he be
able to meet them on their own ground.

"But has God provided one so qualified? Who
is he? Thou art the man! God has given you a
measure of loving faith, and a single eye to His glory.
He has given you some knowledge of men and things,
particularly of the old plan of Methodism. You are
blessed with some health, activity, and diligence,
together with a degree of learning. And to these
He has lately added, by a way none could have foreseen, favour both with the preachers and the whole
people. Come out in the name of God! Come to
the help of the Lord against the mighty! Come while
I am alive and capable of labour;

> '*Dum superest Lachesi quod torqueat, et pedibus me
> Porto meis, nullo dextram subeunte bacillo.*'

Come while I am able, God assisting, to build you up
in faith, to ripen your gifts, and to introduce you to

the people. *Nil tanti.* What possible employment can you have, which is of so great importance?"

When Wesley wrote this letter it was far from his thoughts that he had yet eighteen years of work before him, and would survive Fletcher by six years.

In his reply Fletcher says: " Should Providence call you first, I shall do my best, by the Lord's assistance, to help your brother to gather the wreck, and keep together those who are not absolutely bent to throw away the Methodist doctrine and discipline. . . .

" In the meantime you sometimes need an assistant to serve tables, and occasionally to fill up a gap. Providence visibly appointed *me* to that office many years ago. And though it no less evidently called me hither, yet have I not been without doubt, especially for some years past, whether it would not be expedient that I should resume my office as your deacon; not with any view of presiding over the Methodists after you, but to ease you in your old age, and to be in the way of recovery, and perhaps doing more good. . . .

" Nevertheless, I would not leave this place, without a fuller persuasion that the time is quite come."

Nothing further appears to have been said on the subject, and before long the increasing feebleness of Fletcher's health put the matter beyond discussion.

Two and a half years later Wesley was taken seriously ill while travelling in Ireland. His friends in London were hourly expecting to hear of his death. Charles

Wesley, full of distress, wrote to Fletcher, apparently requesting him to come to London. This Fletcher gently but decidedly declined to do :

"Should your brother fail on earth, you are called, not only to bear up under the loss of so near a relative, but, for the sake of your common children in the Lord, you should endeavour to fill up the gap according to your strength. The Methodists will not expect from you your brother's labours ; but they have, I think, a right to expect that you will preside over them while God spares you in the land of the living. . . . And if at any time you should want my mite of assistance, I hope I shall throw it into the treasury with the simplicity and readiness of the poor widow."

But Wesley recovered, and the call for Fletcher's services never came. Wesley's opinion however remained unaltered, that it would have been better in every way for Fletcher to have joined him in itinerating. Years afterwards, when Fletcher was dead, he wrote :

"I can never believe it was the will of God that such a burning and shining light should be hid under a bushel. No ; instead of being confined to a country village, it ought to have shone in every corner of our land. He was full as much called to sound an alarm through all the nation as Mr. Whitefield himself ; nay, abundantly more so, seeing he was far better qualified for that important work. He had a more striking person, equally good breeding, an equally winning address, together with a richer flow of fancy, a stronger understanding, a far greater treasure of learn-

ing, both in languages, philosophy, philology, and
divinity; and, above all (which I can speak with
fuller assurance, because I had a thorough knowledge
both of one and the other), a more deep and constant
communion with the Father and with the Son Jesus
Christ.

"And yet let not any one imagine that I depreciate
Mr. Whitefield, or undervalue the grace of God and the
extraordinary gifts which his great Master vouchsafed
unto him. I believe he was highly favoured of God;
yea, that he was one of the most eminent ministers
that has appeared in England, or perhaps in the world,
during the present century. Yet I must own I have
known many fully equal to Mr. Whitefield, both in holy
tempers and holiness of conversation; but one equal
herein to Mr. Fletcher I have not known, no, not in a
life of fourscore years."

It was, further, Wesley's belief that an itinerant life
would improve Fletcher's health, which was now seriously affected. His letters had for some time contained
allusions to frequent infirmities. To one correspondent
he says: "My throat is not formed for the labours of
preaching. When I have preached three or four times
together, it inflames and fills up; and the efforts which
I am then obliged to make heat my blood."

To the same, a few months later: "Oh, how life
goes! I walked, now I gallop into eternity. The bowl
of life goes rapidly down the steep hill of time." To
Charles Wesley he writes: "Old age comes faster upon
me than upon you. I am already so gray-headed, that

I wrote to my brother to know if I am not fifty-six instead of forty-six. . . . I have had for some days the symptoms of an inward consumptive decay, spitting blood, etc. Thank God ! I look at our last enemy with great calmness." Wesley confidently recommended a remedy of which he had more experience than any man then living in England, viz. a long journey on horseback. He proposed that Fletcher should accompany him on a journey of some months, telling him, "When you are tired, or like it best, you may come into my carriage ; but remember that riding on horseback is the best of all exercises for you, so far as your strength will permit." Fletcher willingly accepted the proposal, and travelled with Wesley nearly 1200 miles. But after a while certain friends ("kind, but injudicious," Wesley calls them) persuaded him to remain at Stoke Newington, that he might be properly nursed, and have the best medical aid that could be procured. Wesley characteristically remarks, "I verily believe, if he had travelled with me, partly in the chaise and partly on horseback, only a few months longer, he would have quite recovered his health." We are constrained to think that Fletcher was not in a condition to profit by his friend's heroic remedies. He was indeed very ill. Earnest prayers for his recovery were offered at Madeley and elsewhere. A hymn which was composed for the occasion, and sung with deep feeling in Madeley church, contains the following lines :

" Restore him, sinking to the grave ;
Stretch out Thy arm, make haste to save ;

> Back to our hopes and wishes give,
> And bid our friend and father live."

For several months he was under the care of his faithful friends Mr. and Mrs. Greenwood, of Stoke Newington. Rest and silence were enjoined, but it was found impossible to restrain him altogether from speaking. One who was much with him says : "The fire which continually burned in his heart many waters could not quench. It often burst out unawares. And then how did we wonder (like those who formerly heard his Lord) 'at the gracious words which proceeded out of his mouth.' . . .

"It was in these favoured moments of converse that we found, in a particular manner, the reward which is annexed to receiving a prophet in the name of a prophet. And in some of these he mentioned circumstances which, as none knew them but himself, would otherwise have been buried in oblivion.

"One of these remarkable passages was, 'In the beginning,' said he, 'of my spiritual course, I heard the voice of God, in an articulate, but inexpressibly awful, sound, go through my soul in those words : "*If any man will be My disciple, let him deny himself.*"' He mentioned another peculiar manifestation of a later date, 'in which, said he, 'I was favoured, like Moses, with a supernatural discovery of the glory of God, in an ineffable converse with Him, face to face ; so that, whether I was in the body or out of the body, I cannot tell.'

"At another time he said, 'About the time of my entering into the ministry, I one evening wandered into a wood, musing on the importance of the office I was going to undertake. I then began to pour out my soul in prayer; when such a sense of the justice of God fell upon me, and such a sense of His displeasure at sin, as absorbed all my powers, and filled my soul with the agony of prayer for poor, lost sinners. I continued therein till the dawn of day; and I considered this as designed of God to impress upon me more deeply the meaning of those solemn words, Knowing therefore the terror of the Lord, we persuade men.'"

Throughout the whole of his long illness Fletcher's spirit was, not only calm and tranquil, but attuned to an ardour and heavenliness that deeply impressed all who saw him. His frail body seemed to be the abode of a spirit purified and perfected till every trace of earthly corruption was lost.

During the months of enforced absence from his parish his heart was still with his people. In a pastoral letter, which is dated Newington, December 28th, 1776, he writes:

"I hoped to have spent the Christmas holidays with you, and to have ministered to you in holy things; but the weakness of my body confining me here, I humbly submit to the Divine dispensation. . . . The sum of all I have preached to you is contained in four propositions. *First*, heartily repent of your sins, original and actual. *Secondly*, believe the gospel of Christ in sincerity and truth. *Thirdly*, in the power which true faith gives, run the way of God's commandments before God and men. *Fourthly*, by continuing to take up your cross, and to receive the pure milk of God's word, grow in grace, and in the knowledge of Jesus Christ.   .   .   .

" The more nearly I consider death and the grave, judgment and eternity, the more I feel that I have preached to you the truth, and that the truth is solid as the Rock of ages.   Although I hope to see much more of the goodness of the Lord in the land of the living than I do see, yet, blessed be the Divine mercy ! I see enough to keep my mind at all times unruffled, and to make me willing calmly to resign my soul into the hands of my faithful Creator, my loving Redeemer, and my sanctifying Comforter, *this moment*, or *the next*, if He calls for it."

Fletcher's almsgiving was proportionate with his prayers.   He was in receipt of an income from his little property in Switzerland of about £100 a year. He generally gave it all away.   His money, his clothes, his furniture were alike at the service of the poor and suffering.   At one time he sends back £80 to Switzerland for distribution among the poor, saying, " As money is rather higher there than here the mite will go further abroad than it would in my parish."   At another time he deposited £105 with a friend, but the whole was drawn for charitable purposes in a few months, the balance, which was £24, going to complete the preaching-house he had built at Madeley Wood. During his illness he writes to one of the poor Methodists at Coalbrookdale : " Let none of your little companies want.   If any do, you are welcome to my house. Take any part of the furniture there, and make use of it for their relief. And this shall be your full title for so doing. Witness my hand, JOHN FLETCHER."

Leaving Stoke Newington in the beginning of May, 1777, Fletcher went to Bristol, to the hospitable home of his old friend Mr. Ireland, for change of air, and for what benefit might be found in drinking the waters. Here he spent several months in feeble health, but in unbroken tranquillity and elevation of spirit. "Far gone in a consumptive disorder, and ripening fast for glory," was the judgment of those who saw him at this time. He had many visitors, devout persons of all classes, to whom his conversation, his prayers, his very presence, were means of grace. Mr. Venn, who had been on the opposite side to Fletcher in the recent controversy, spent some weeks with him under Mr. Ireland's roof. "Oh that I might be like him!" was his testimony in after years. " I have known all the great men for these fifty years, but I have known none like him. . . . I never heard him say a single word which was not proper to be spoken, and which had not a tendency to minister grace to the hearers; . . . not a single unbecoming word of himself, or of his antagonists, or of his friends. All his conversation tended to excite to greater love and thankfulness for the benefits of redemption ; whilst his whole deportment breathed humility and love."

In the month of July Wesley and his preachers met in Bristol to hold their annual conference. One morning during its session a visit from Fletcher was announced. As he entered what was then called the New

K

Room—now the old chapel in Broadmead—leaning on
Mr. Ireland's arm, the whole assembly, by a common
impulse, stood up. Wesley rose and advanced to receive
him. He seemed like a visitor from another world.
His worn features shone as with the light of heaven.
All present were profoundly moved at the sight. He
had scarcely begun to speak before every one was in
tears. "His appearance, his exhortations, and his
prayers," says Benson, "broke most of our hearts."
It was such a scene as the oldest person present had
never witnessed before, as the youngest could not expect to witness again. It was brought to a close by
Wesley, who suddenly fell upon his knees at Fletcher's
side, the whole company of preachers kneeling with him,
and offered an earnest prayer for Fletcher's restora-
tion to health and to his labours in the cause of Christ.
He finished his prayer by pronouncing "in his peculiar
manner, and with a confidence and emphasis which
seemed to thrill through every heart, 'He shall not die,
but live, and declare the works of the Lord.'"

During the eight remaining years of Fletcher's life, it
was believed amongst the Methodists that God had
spared him in answer to their prayers.

CHAPTER X.

RESIDENCE IN SWITZERLAND.

AFTER spending some months at Bristol, with little, if any, improvement in his health, Fletcher was strongly urged to spend the winter abroad. The south of France, and Spain were both suggested, and his brothers and sisters in Switzerland sent him a pressing invitation to revisit his home, and breathe once more his native air. He yielded at last to the advice of physicians and friends, and made the necessary arrangements for a long absence from Madeley. His curate, Mr. Greaves, who had supplied his place for some months, was to remain in charge of the parish. The vicar's income was assigned, part to Mr. Greaves, and the rest to the maintenance of various good works in and around Madeley.

Before setting out on his journey he addressed a pastoral letter "To the Brethren who hear the Word of God in the Parish Church of Madeley." It was full of affectionate counsels and exhortations. In bidding them farewell, he writes: "I hope to see you again in the flesh; but my sweetest and firmest hope is to meet you where there are no parting seas, no interposing mountains, no sickness, no death, no fear of loving too much, no shame for loving too little."

On December 4th, 1777, after being delayed at Dover for a day or two by bad weather, Fletcher crossed the Channel with Mr. Ireland and his two daughters, who were desirous of spending the winter in the south, and of ministering to the comfort of their loved and honoured friend.

He remained abroad for nearly three years and a half. This period of seclusion and comparative inactivity is full of interest to the student of Fletcher's history. It is true we lose sight of him for months together, and find it difficult to weave into a consistent story the references to persons and places which are to be found in his letters, and in sundry narratives that have come down to us; but the change of scene and circumstance gives additional charm to the portraiture of his gentle life. It must not be forgotten that Fletcher, though almost more English than the English themselves in his attachment to the institutions of this country, was a Swiss, and we cannot desire that the Swiss in him should be suppressed; we would not have him "forget his own people and his father's house." Away from Madeley, from the Church of England, from Methodism, he moves amid moral and social surroundings which were, after all, native to him, and amongst which his character could not but reveal some aspects not similarly brought out by his life in England. These years spent in France and Switzerland add to the moral picturesqueness of his course as a whole.

The route taken by Fletcher and his friends was by Calais, Abbeville, etc., to Dijon and Lyons, and thence to Aix in Provence, where they remained for some time. They afterwards visited Montpellier, Marseilles, and Hyères, though in what order it is difficult to determine, and in the spring of 1778 Fletcher reached Nyon, where he was to spend the next three years. This outline of his journeyings may now be supplemented by extracts from his letters and those of his companions.

"When we departed from Calais," writes Mr. Ireland, "the north wind was very high, and penetrated us even in the chaise. We put up in Breteuil, and the next day got to Abbeville, whence we were forced, by the miserable accommodation we met with, to set out, though it was Sunday. Hitherto Mr. Fletcher and I had led the way, but now the other chaises got before us. Nine miles from Abbeville our axletree gave way through the hard frost, and we were left to the piercing cold on the side of a hill without shelter. After waiting an hour and a half, we sent the axletree and wheels back to be repaired; and, leaving the body of the chaise under a guard, procured another to carry us to the next town. On the 15th our chaise arrived in good repair. The country was covered with snow, but travelling steadily forward, we reached Dijon on the 27th. During the whole journey Mr. Fletcher showed marks of recovery. He bore both the fatigue and cold as well as the best of us. On the 31st we put up at Lyons, and solemnly closed the year, bowing our knees before the throne, which indeed we did all together every day. January 4th, 1778, we left Lyons, and came on the 9th to Aix. Here we rest, the weather being exceedingly fine and warm. Mr.

Fletcher walks out daily. He is now able to read and pray with us every morning and evening. He has no remains of his cough nor of the weakness in his breast. His natural colour is restored, and the sallowness is quite gone. His appetite is good, and he takes a little wine."

In another letter, written from Aix, he says : " Soon after our arrival here, I rode out most days with my dear and valued friend. Now and then he complained of the uneasiness of the horse, and there were some remains of soreness in his breast, but this soon went off. The beginning of February was warm, and the warmth, when he walked in the fields, relaxed him ; but when the wind got north or east, he was braced again. His appetite is good, his complexion as healthy as it was eleven years ago. As his strength increases he increases the length of his rides. Last Tuesday he set out on a journey of a hundred and twelve miles. The first day he travelled forty miles without feeling any fatigue, and the third day fifty-five. He bore the journey as well as I did, and was as well and as active at the end of it as at the beginning. During the day he cried out, ' Help me to praise the Lord for His goodness ; I never expected to see this day.' He accepted a pressing invitation to preach to the Protestants here ; and he fulfilled his engagement on Sunday morning, taking as his text, ' Examine yourselves, whether ye be in the faith.' Both the French and English were greatly affected ; the word went to the hearts of both saints and sinners. His voice is now as good as ever it was, and he has an earnest invitation to preach near Montpellier, where we are going. You would be astonished at the entreaties of pastors as well as people. He has received a letter from a minister in the Levine Mountains, who intends to come to Montpellier, sixty miles, to press him to go and preach to his flock. He purposes to spend the next summer in his own country, and the following winter in these parts."

From Montpellier Fletcher wrote to his curate, Mr. Greaves: "Please God, I shall set out next week from this place, where the winter has been uncommonly rainy and windy. We had over half an inch of snow last week, but it was gone long before noon. The climate has, nevertheless, agreed with me better than England, and as a proof of it, I need only tell you that I rode last Friday from Hyères, the orange gardens of France, hither, which is near fifty miles, and was well enough to preach last Sunday, in French, at the Protestant chapel. . . . At the first convenient opportunity, please to read the following note in the church: John Fletcher sends his best Christian love to the congregation that worships God in the parish church at Madeley. He begs the continuance of their prayers for strength of body and mind, that he may be able (if it be the will of God) to serve them again in the gospel. He desires them to return Almighty God thanks for having enabled him to speak again in public last Sunday, without having had a return of his spitting of blood, which he considers as a token that his life may be spared a little, to exhort them to grow in grace, in the knowledge of our Lord Jesus Christ, and in brotherly love;—the best marks that we know God, and are in the faith of Christ."

Early in May he reached Nyon, having travelled under the care of his brother from Montpellier. He was received by the members of his family with the utmost affection and respect.

One of the most important letters which he wrote during his absence from England was addressed to "The Rev. Messrs. John and Charles Wesley." It is dated from Macon in Burgundy, May 17th, 1778. The following extracts will show Fletcher's judgment concerning the state of morals and religion in France ten years before the Revolution :

"Gambling and dress, sinful pleasure and love ot money, unbelief and false philosophy, lightness of spirit, fear of man, and love of the world, are the principal sins by which Satan binds his captives in these parts. Materialism is not rare; deism and Socinianism are very common ; and a set of freethinkers, great admirers of Voltaire and Rousseau, Bayle and Mirabeau, seem bent upon destroying Christianity and government. If we believe them, the world is the dupe of kings and priests; religion is fanaticism and superstition; subordination is slavery ; Christian morality is absurd, unnatural, and impracticable ; and Christianity the most bloody religion that ever was. And here it is certain, that by the example of Christians *so called*, and by our continual disputes, they have a great advantage, and do the truth immense mischief. *Popery will certainly fall in France, in this or the next century ;* and I have no doubt God will use those vain men to bring about a reformation here, as he used Henry the Eighth to do that work in

England; so the madness of His enemies shall, at last, turn to His praise, and to the furtherance of His kingdom. . . .

"If you ask, what system these men adopt, I answer, Some build on deism a morality founded on *self-preservation, self-interest,* and *self-honour;* others laugh at all morality, except that which being neglected *violently* disturbs society. And external order is the decent covering of fatalism, while materialism is their system.

"Oh! dear sirs, let me entreat you, in these dangerous days, to use your wide influence, with unabated zeal, against the scheme of these modern Celsuses, Porphyries, and Julians, by calling all professors to think and speak the same things, to love and embrace one another, and to firmly resist those daring men, many of whom are already in England, headed by the admirers of Mr. Hume and Mr. Hobbes. But it is needless to say this to those who have made, and continue to make, such a stand for vital Christianity, so that I have nothing to do but pray that the Lord may abundantly support and strengthen you, and make you a continued comfort to His enlightened people, loving reprovers of those who mix light with darkness, and a terror to the perverse."

While residing at Nyon Fletcher was visited by his friend and former medical adviser, William Perronet, son of the venerable Vicar of Shoreham. The Perronet family was of Swiss origin, and about this time it came to the knowledge of Mr. Perronet that he had some claim to a property situated at Chateau d'Œx, a small town in a mountain valley, about twenty miles from the north-eastern shore of the Lake of Geneva, and nearly sixty from Nyon. Fletcher assisted his friends by making inquiries and obtaining legal advice, and it was thought necessary that William Perronet should go over to press the claim in person. This he accordingly did, and, it may be said here, with complete success, though he did not live to enjoy the possession, as he was taken ill on his way home, and died before reaching England.

Fletcher wrote, inviting him to be his guest : " This is a delightful country. If you come to see it, and to claim the estate, bring all the papers and letters you can collect ; and share a pleasant apartment, and one of the finest prospects in the world, in the house where I was born."

Soon after Mr. Perronet's arrival, it was thought necessary that he should visit Chateau d'Œx, and although it was now December, Fletcher accompanied him. The journey was not without danger, more especially for one in such a feeble state of health. It is described, together with many interesting details of Fletcher's life at Nyon, in Mr. Perronet's letters.

" On Friday, the 11th, I reached Nyon, where I had the pleasure of finding our dear friend in pretty good health and spirits. Mr. Fletcher's house is a fine, large building, agreeably situated. It is in the form of a castle, and is supposed to have been built five hundred years ago. . . .

" His chief delight seems to be in the meeting of his little society of children; and as he is exceedingly fond of them, they appear to be altogether as fond of him. He seldom either walks abroad or rides out, but some of them follow him, singing the hymns they have learned, and conversing with him by the way. But you must not suppose that he is permitted to enjoy this happiness unmolested. Not only the drunkards make songs upon him and his little companions, but many of the clergy loudly complain of such irregular proceedings."

Mr. Perronet was much impressed with the incidents of their journey to Chateau d'Œx. The rugged heights, the precipices, the torrents, the deep snow, rising many feet above their heads as they toiled through narrow passes that had been cut through it,—all are new to him, and are described with much vivacity. Part of the distance they rode upon a sledge, and in some places they were obliged to go on foot. Whilst doing so they got a fall on the ice, when Fletcher received a severe blow on the back of his head, and his companion sprained his wrist. Though they only spent two days at Chateau d'Œx, Fletcher was constrained to preach the gospel to the people. He was visited by some of the principal inhabitants, who stood round him in deep attention for nearly an hour while he exhorted and prayed.

As his strength permitted, Fletcher laboured, not only in Nyon, but, true to the Methodist principles he had learnt in England, made journeys in various directions, that he might scatter the good seed. Amongst the Jura Mountains he found industrious and thriving populations. In one village they told him they had the best

singing, and the best preacher in the country. But when
he asked if any sinners were converted under his ministry, they stared, and asked what he meant. When he
had explained himself, they could only say, " We do not
live in the time of miracles." Having crossed into
French territory, he was much interested on coming
upon a great gathering of people who were assembled
to hear some itinerant mission preachers, Roman Catholic clergymen. They were, it appears, three brothers,
and they had already spent some days in the place,
preaching morning and evening. Fletcher heard one of
them preach upon the judgment. " Before the sermon,
all those who, for the press, could kneel, did, and sang
a French hymn to beg a blessing on the word ; and indeed it was blessed. An awful attention was visible
upon most, and, during a good part of the discourse, the
voice of the preacher was almost lost in the cries and
bitter wailings of the audience." The preacher urged
them to know their day, and slight the mercy of God
and the blood of Christ no longer ; and Fletcher adds,
" I have seen but once or twice congregations so much
affected in England."

Devout and earnest Roman Catholics were much
more to his mind than formal, lifeless Protestants. On
Good Friday, which was not observed amongst the
Calvinists of Nyon, Fletcher and Mr. Perronet crossed
the lake into Savoy to hear a celebrated Capuchin
preacher. Fletcher was much pleased with his discourse, and spent two or three hours with him and his
brethren in serious and friendly conversation.

To many of the Swiss ministers his "irregularities" were as distasteful as such things were to the "high" or "moderate" clergy in England. His earnestness and popularity perplexed them. The people crowded the churches where he preached, multitudes who could not gain admittance remaining outside, while others placed ladders against the windows, and climbed to places whence they might hear, even if they could not see him. Pulpits to which he had been at first invited were closed against him. It was represented to the authorities that he preached doctrines subversive of morality and social order, and that on this account he had been banished from England. At a visitation held in Nyon strong complaints were made against him, the ministers of the town, however, taking his part, while those of Geneva and Lausanne were opposed to him. He was forbidden to hold meetings in private houses, and householders were warned that they would be liable to penalties if they permitted such meetings to be held. This roused the spirit of his brother, who wrote to the *Bailli* saying that he would give up neither his civil nor religious liberty, and would open his house for the word of God. But the climax was reached when Fletcher was summoned before the *Bailli*, who sharply reprimanded him for preaching against Sabbath-breaking and stage plays. The former, he said, implied a censure on the magistrates in general, as if they neglected their duty; and the latter he considered as a personal reflection on himself, he having just invited a company of French comedians to Nyon. Accordingly, he forbade him any longer to exercise any of the functions of a minister in the country. Fletcher, however, still found means to catechize the children and to hold meetings in private. At the same time he was informed that if he would renounce his ordination, and obtain Presbyterian orders, he would be allowed to preach, and on those terms a minister in Nyon offered him what might be called a curacy.

The following extracts from his letters, written while at Nyon, will throw light both upon the state of things there, and upon his occupations and sentiments at this time.

July 15th, 1778.—"The day I preached, I met with some children in my wood, walking or gathering strawberries. I spoke to them about our Father, our common Father. They said they would sing to their Father as well as the birds, and followed me, attempting to make such melody as you know is commonly made in these parts. I outrode them, but some of them had the patience to follow me home, and said they would speak with me ; but the people of the house stopped them, saying, I could not be troubled with children. They cried, and said they were sure I would not say so, for I was their good brother. The next day, when I heard it, I inquired after them, and invited them to come to me, which they have done every day since. I make them little hymns which they sing. . . . Last Sunday I met them in the wood : there were a hundred of them, and as many adults. Our first pastor has since desired me to desist from preaching in the wood, . . .

and I have complied, from a concurrence of circumstances which are not worth mentioning. I therefore meet them in my father's yard."

Sept. 17*th*, 1778.—"One of our ministers being ill, I ventured a second time into the pulpit last Sunday; and the Sunday before I preached six miles off to two thousand people in a jail-yard, where they were come to see a poor murderer two days before his execution. I was a little abused by the Bailiff on the occasion, and refused the liberty of attending the poor man on the scaffold, where he was to be broken on the wheel. I hope he died penitent."

Feb. 2*nd*, 1779.—"I am better, thank God! and ride out every day when the slippery roads will permit me to venture without the risk of breaking my horse's legs, and my own neck. You will ask me how I have spent my time. I pray, have patience, rejoice, and write when I can. I saw wood in the house when I cannot go out, and eat grapes, of which I have always a basket by me. . . .

"The truths I chiefly insist upon, when I talk to the people who will hear me, are those which I feed upon myself, as my daily bread: God, our Maker and Preserver, though invisible, is here and everywhere. He is our chief good, because all beauty and all goodness centres in and flows from Him. He is especially love: and love in us, being His image, is the sum and substance of all moral and spiritual excellence,—of all true and lasting bliss. In Adam we are all estranged from love and from God; but the second Adam, Jesus,

Emmanuel, God with us, is come to make us know and enjoy again our God as the God of love and the chief good. All who receive Jesus receive power to become the sons of God, etc., etc."

March 7th, 1780.—"I am sorry the building has come to so much more than I intended; but as the mischief is done, it is a matter to exercise patience, resignation, and self-denial; and it will be a caution in future. I am going to sell part of my little estate here to discharge the debt. I had laid by £50 to print a small work, which I wanted to distribute here; but, as I must be just before I presume to offer that mite to the God of truth, I lay by the design, and shall send that sum to Mr. York. Money is so scarce here at this time that I shall sell at very great loss; but necessity and justice are two great laws which must be obeyed. As I design on my return to England to pinch until I have got rid of this debt, I may go and live in one of the cottages belonging to the vicar, if we could let the vicarage for a few pounds."

Sept. 15*th*, 1780.—"There is little genuine piety in these parts: nevertheless, there is yet some of the form of it; so far as to go to the Lord's table regularly four times a year. There meet the adulterers, the drunkards, the swearers, the infidels, and even the materialists. They have no idea of the double damnation that awaits hypocrites. They look upon partaking that sacrament as a ceremony enjoined by the magistrate."

Feb. 14*th*, 1781.—"My friend Ireland invites me to join him in the south of France, and I long to see whether I could not have more liberty to preach the word among Papists than among Protestants. But it is so little that I can do, that I doubt much whether it is worth while going so far upon so little a chance. If I were stronger, and had more time, the fear of being hanged should not detain me."

It had occurred to Fletcher during his residence in Nyon that he might serve the cause of religion in Switzerland with his pen, seeing that the state of his health, and the opposition of persons in authority, made it impossible for him to preach the gospel, as it was in his heart to do. To awaken the clergy, to rouse them from their worldliness and scepticism, and bring them to some acquaintance with true religion, seemed of all things the most desirable. Humanly speaking, there was little hope for the Church in Switzerland until there was, at least, the leaven of an earnest ministry. To his friend and curate at Madeley, Mr. Greaves, he wrote: "There is occasion and great need to bear a testimony against the faults of the clergy here; and if I cannot do it from the pulpit, I must try to do it from the press. Their canons, which were composed by two hundred and thirty pastors at the time of the Reformation, are so spiritual and apostolic that I design to translate them into English, if I am spared."

It does not appear that this design was carried out, but meanwhile Fletcher was preparing a practical treatise on the " Pastoral Character," which he hoped to publish before leaving the country. It grew upon his hands into a lengthy and elaborate work. His plan was

L

to exhibit at one view the character of the primitive
Christian, and of the apostolic minister, as exemplified
in the Apostle Paul. It was written in French, but
was still unfinished when he returned to England, and
the manuscript was laid aside, with the intention of
translating and preparing it for the press when circumstances should allow. The convenient season, however,
did not come, and it was not until after his death that
the manuscript was found—portions of it from time to
time,—obviously needing revision at the author's hand.
The task of translating and editing was performed by
the Rev. Joshua Gilpin, and his version of " The Portrait of St. Paul " is the only one that has ever appeared. No mode of publication could well be more
disadvantageous to a writer, and this should be borne
in mind in estimating its value. Mr. Gilpin remarks
that " the manuscript was so incorrect and confused as
frequently to stagger the resolution of the translator " ;
and as his object was rather to produce an edifying
work than to edit with precision Fletcher's literary remains, it is probable that he filled up the gaps and
elaborated the hints which he found in Fletcher's
papers. This would in part account for the diffuseness
which characterises " The Portrait of St. Paul." The
tendency, so frequently discernible in Fletcher's writings,
is here most conspicuous. In the first division of the
work the moral character of St. Paul is delineated under
no less than forty " Traits," each one having a chapter
to itself, the chapters being numbered successively
TRAIT 1, TRAIT 2, and so on, to forty. Had Fletcher

completed this treatise, and published it himself, it is
reasonable to believe that his own literary experience or
the advice of his friends would have led him to group
these numerous details under fewer heads, and in other
ways give greater unity to the .whole. There is hardly
a chapter that does not show the writer's spiritual insight and experience, and may not be read with profit,
even by those who are acquainted with the best works of
pastoral theology ; but the cataloguing of moral features
is carried to a fatiguing length, and the portrait which
it was intended to exhibit is in danger of disappearing
in the process of linked and long-drawn description.

Even in its present form it is not difficult to see that
the " Portrait of St. Paul " was written by one who had
Swiss readers in view. The authors most frequently
quoted are Ostervald, professor and pastor at Neuf-
chatel, whose " Exercice du Ministère Sacré " was published in 1739, and Roques, formerly minister of the
French congregation at Basle, whose " Pasteur Evan-
gélique," published in 1723, was still a popular work.
It was an advantage for Fletcher to be able to appeal
to " such excellent and learned divines as Mons. Ostervald and Mons. Roques " in setting forth the character
and calling of the Christian minister.

The third and concluding portion of the work is " An
Essay on the Connexion of Doctrines and Morality." It
might almost be considered a separate and independent
work. Its object is to show the insufficiency of natural
religion and philosophy to produce true goodness. We
are reminded on every page that it was written in the

country of Rousseau's birth and of Voltaire's adoption, at a time when the wit of the one, the sentiment of the other, and the principles of both these philosophers and men of letters, were of paramount influence in Switzerland. Voltaire and Rousseau died in the year 1778, while Fletcher was residing at Nyon, and he had ample opportunity of observing the extent to which both clergy and laity had come under their spell. That influence was, in Fletcher's judgment, the cause of grievous injury to religion and morals. A loose, easy-going, yet confident deism seemed almost to have superseded Christianity. Even amongst the clergy the truth of revelation was denied, or its importance disparaged. The doctrines of revealed religion were ridiculed as mysterious and incredible, or rejected as having no practical bearing. The religion of nature had a showy and pretentious side for those who aspired to the dignity of philosophers, and was easily reconcilable with selfishness, vanity, and licentiousness alike in its more, and in its less, illustrious professors.

Fletcher set himself to show the relation between principles and conduct, and particularly between the doctrines of the gospel and a pure morality, instituting comparisons between Christianity and the current deism in respect of their ethical force and direction .His references to Rousseau are frequent, as might be expected, and it was not difficult for so expert a controversialist to give a good account of the author of *Émile.* The "Confessions" of Rousseau were not published until 1782, four years after his death; but Fletcher lived in a country where Rousseau's history and character were well known. The most direct allusion, however, to his personal qualities occurs in the following passage, taken from the close of the treatise :

"If it be asked, what secret vice it was that would not suffer so honest a man as J. J. Rousseau to embrace the gospel, without searching into the anecdotes of his life, we may rest satisfied with the discovery he has made of his own heart in this single sentence : 'What can be more transporting to a noble soul than the pride of virtue !' Such was the pride which made him vainly presume that he had power sufficient to conquer himself, without invoking the assistance of God; and by which he was encouraged to assert that the doctrines of the gospel were such as 'no sensible man could either conceive or admit.'

"There is no species of pride more insolent than that which gives rise to the following language : 'It is asserted that "God so loved the world, as to give His only begotten Son, that whosoever believeth in Him should not perish, but have everlasting life." These tidings, whether they be true or false, are highly acceptable to many; but for my own part, I openly declare that I reject with contempt the idea of such a favour. I read with attention those writings which tend to unfold the mysteries of nature, but resolve never to turn over those authors who vainly attempt to establish the truth of the gospel. This subject, though it has occupied the thoughts and engaged the pens of inquiring students for these seventeen hundred years, I shall

ever regard as unworthy my attention. I leave it to the
vulgar, who are easily persuaded of its importance. My
virtues are sufficient to expiate my crimes, and on these
I will resolutely depend, as my sole mediators before
God.' . . .

"The deists of Socrates' time must have been far less
culpable than those of the present day. The former,
conscious of the uncertainty with which they were encompassed, made use of every help they could procure
in the pursuit of truth with unwearied assiduity. The
latter, presuming upon their own sufficiency, decide
against doctrines of the utmost importance without
impartially considering the evidence produced in their
favour. The former, by carefully examining every
system of morality proposed to their deliberation, discovered a candour and liberality becoming those who
were anxiously 'feeling after God, if haply they might
find Him.' The latter, by condemning revelation without calmly attending to the arguments of its advocates,
manifest a degree of prejudice that would be unpardon-
able in a judge, but which becomes inexcusable in a
criminal, who is pressed by the strongest reasons to
search out the truth."

On his return to England, Fletcher brought this unfinished treatise with him, and, as we have said, never
found time to complete it. One work he published
while in Switzerland, a poem entitled "La Louange,"
afterwards enlarged and republished in England under
the title, "La Grace et La Nature." The Swiss edition
required, and received, the license of the official censor

at Lausanne, who was good enough to give his impri-
matur in the following terms: "I have read this work,
which, in my judgment, everywhere breathes Piety,
Faith, and Christian Charity."—DE BONS, *Censeur.* The
English edition was dedicated, by permission, to Queen
Charlotte.

One incident connected with Fletcher's residence at
Nyon remains to be told. A certain nephew of his,
lately an officer in the Sardinian army, had been compelled to leave the service under discreditable circumstances. To rid themselves of his company, his brother
officers agreed to challenge him in succession. After
fighting two or three duels, he was obliged to resign his
commission and leave the country. He returned to
Switzerland, to become a terror and a distress to his
relatives. Having squandered his money in various evil
ways, and come to the end of his resources, he resorted
to a desperate expedient. He asked for a private interview with his uncle, General de Gons, and when they
were alone, suddenly presented a loaded pistol, and
said, " Uncle de Gons, if you do not give me a draft on
your banker for five hundred crowns, I will shoot you."
His uncle, finding himself in the power of a desperado
capable of any mischief, and, possibly, having no heart
to resist the violence of one who was all but a son,
complied with his demand. His nephew then extracted
a promise from him that he would not, on his honour as
a gentleman and a soldier, take any steps to recover the
draft, or bring him to justice; after which he rode off
triumphant with his ill-gotten gains.

As he passed the door of his uncle Fletcher, the
fancy took him to call and pay him a visit, and he
began at once to tell him of the kindness of his uncle
De Gons, who had just given him five hundred crowns,
adding, as he held out the draft, "If you don't believe
me, see the proof under his own hand." Fletcher felt
that there was something wrong.   He took the draft,
and looked first at it, and then at the young man.   "It
is, indeed, my brother's writing," said he, "and I am
astonished to see it, for he is not rich, and I know that
he so much disapproves your conduct that you are the
last of the family to whom he would make such a present." Then folding the paper, and putting it into his
pocket, he added, "It strikes me, young man, that you
have come by this by some improper means, and I
cannot, in honesty, return it to you but with my brother's
knowledge and approbation."   Out came the young
ruffian's pistol once more, and putting it to Fletcher's
breast, he swore he would have his life if he did not
immediately return him the draft.   "My life," replied
Fletcher, "is secure in the hands of God."   The young
man still sought to terrify him into compliance.   "Do
you think," said Fletcher, "that I have been twenty-five
years the minister of the Lord of life, to be afraid of
death now?   It is for you to fear death, who have every
reason to fear it.   You are a gambler and a cheat, yet
call yourself a gentleman !   You are a seducer, and a
duellist, and call yourself a man of honour !   Look
there, sir; look there !   The eye of God is upon us.
Tremble in the presence of your Maker, who can in a

moment kill your body, and for ever punish your soul in hell."

The young man was powerless. He stormed and trembled alternately. He withdrew his pistol, and again presented it. He argued, entreated, threatened, but Fletcher remained calm and fearless. By-and-by he expostulated with him. "I cannot," said he, "return my brother's draft; yet I am sorry for you, and will do what I can to help you. General de Gons will, at my request, I am sure, give you a hundred crowns. I will do the same. Perhaps my brother Henry will do as much; and perhaps the other members of the family will make up the sum amongst them." He then knelt down, and prayed for his unhappy nephew. The matter was arranged, by Fletcher's influence, in the way he had suggested, and an opportunity was afforded to a foolish and wicked young man for repentance and reformation of life.

FLETCHER returned to England in the spring of 1781, after an absence of nearly three years and a half. His health was considerably improved by the long rest and retirement; the worst symptoms had disappeared, but he remained, at best, a frail and delicate man.

Almost his first act on reaching London was to preach in the new chapel in City Road, which had been erected during his absence. Wesley was away in the midland counties, preaching and visiting the societies; from thence he passed into Wales, and next to the Isle of Man, so that some months elapsed before he and Fletcher met. After a few days in London Fletcher went to Bristol, where he received the warmest welcome from Mr. Ireland and his other friends. Soon after his arrival, Mr. Rankin, a Methodist preacher then stationed in Bristol, had an interview with him, "which," he says, "I shall never forget in time or eternity." Fletcher had many inquiries to make concerning the progress of religion in England and in America, where Mr. Rankin had laboured for five years. They walked to and fro in Mr. Ireland's garden, and as he listened to Mr. Rankin's account of the triumphs of the gospel at home and in the colonies, Fletcher broke forth again and again into prayer and praise.

In almost every reference to him at this period of his life, and onward to its close, there is mention of a something almost unearthly in his spirit, and even in his appearance and manner. With the utmost affectionateness and freedom of intercourse there was a certain raptness of devotion, a mingled simplicity and elevation of thought and feeling, peculiarly his own. The impression he produced, as shown in the letters and journals of his contemporaries, is unmistakable. There is nothing quite like it in the case of any other member of the group to which Fletcher belongs. Alike in converse with individuals, and in his public addresses, he gave the impression of one whose links with earth were few and slender compared with those that united him with the heavenly world. After describing the interview just referred to, Mr. Rankin goes on to say: "He preached in the evening from 'God hath from the beginning chosen you to salvation through sanctification of the Spirit and belief of the truth.' The whole congregation was dissolved in tears. He spoke like one who had just left the converse of God and angels, and not like a human being. The different conversations I had with him, his prayers and preaching during the few days which he stayed at Bristol and Brislington, left such an impression on my mind, and were attended with such salutary effects, that for several months afterwards not a cloud intervened between God and my soul,—not for one hour. Of all the men I ever knew, I never saw such love to God and man, such deadness to the world, such entire consecratedness to Jesus, as in him. It often appeared to me that his every breath was prayer and praise. He lived more like a disembodied spirit than a human being."

No one rejoiced at Fletcher's return to England more than his old friend and former colleague at Trevecca, Mr. Benson. In a hitherto unpublished letter, dated from the "Preaching House, Leeds," June 12th, 1781, he wrote to him as follows :

" It gave me great pleasure to hear of your safe arrival in England after so long an absence, and that your health was considerably better than when you went abroad ; and more especially, as I understand from Miss Bosanquet, that you have some thought of visiting Yorkshire, where, I am sure, thousands will be glad to see you, and none more so than myself, who once had the honour of being your intimate friend, and whose one motive for troubling you at this time is a desire to renew that friendship, formerly so beneficial to my soul.

" Mr. Fletcher, no length of time, no distance of place, can ever erase your memory from my mind, nor shall I, while I breathe, cease to respect you above all men upon earth, and that for one *only* reason, because the Lord Jesus Christ has in a great measure drawn His likeness upon you."

Although he returned to Madeley soon after reaching England, it was some time before Fletcher really took up his residence and resumed his work there. He determined to attend the approaching Methodist Conference, to be held in Leeds in the beginning of August. Four years had elapsed since his memorable visit to the Conference at Bristol, when Wesley had said concerning him, "He shall not die, but live." He now wished to meet once more the brethren to whom he was bound by so many ties. Wesley moreover wanted his presence and counsel, and for this, and for another reason that will be explained, he left Madeley and went to Yorkshire.

Seventy preachers met at the Conference. On the Sunday before it began, the Methodists had a high day at the parish church of Leeds. Wesley preached to a vast congregation. Seventeen clergymen, including Fletcher and Coke, assisted him in administering the Lord's supper to eleven hundred communicants. During the Conference Wesley desired Fletcher, Coke, and four others to meet him each evening to consult with him on any difficulty that might occur. Fletcher preached at five o'clock in the morning to at least two thousand persons, who listened to him with the deepest attention. Wesley's comment was, "I do not wonder he should be so popular; not only because he preaches with all his might, but because the power of God attends both his preaching and prayer." "I had the happiness to hear that venerable servant of God, Mr. Fletcher," wrote one of the preachers to his wife. "Never did I see any man more like what I suppose the ancient apostles to have been. . . . I think I never heard a sermon to be compared with it. I wish I could tell you

every word. I had also the happiness to receive from
his hand the bread in the sacrament of the Lord's
supper."

The Conference was over in a week, but Fletcher
still remained in the neighbourhood of Leeds. Another,
and to him a still more important, matter was occupying
his thoughts. It had reference to Miss Bosanquet, the
lady named in Mr. Benson's letter. A very brief account
of one who deserves, and has received, ample biographic
honours, must here suffice. Mary Bosanquet was a
lady of good family and considerable fortune, to whom
belongs an eminence among the godly women of
Methodism, analogous to that of Fletcher among his
associates. At a very early age, and partly through the
influence of a maidservant, she became an earnest
Christian. As she grew up she passed through much
conflict and sorrow from the opposition of her parents.
They were well-meaning but worldly people, and were
disappointed and annoyed at their daughter's distaste for
balls and theatres, and at her generally impracticable
religious convictions. They endeavoured to secure her
promise that she would never, either then or thereafter,
attempt to make her brothers "what she called Christians." Upon her saying that she dared not consent to
that, her father replied, "Then you force me to put
you out of my house." A kind of agreement was soon
afterwards come to, that she should take lodgings in
Hoxton, and visit her parents from time to time ; and
at twenty-one years of age, accompanied by her maid,
she left her home, literally for Christ's sake. A year

or two later she removed to Leytonstone, to a house of her own, not far from her father's residence. Here she gathered around her a family of poor women and orphan children, who were supported at her expense, and taught, trained, and employed according to their capacity. It was her desire to form a household in which the glory of God should be the supreme end and aim, and for many years her efforts were crowned with success. Peace, piety, and simple order ruled the little community. Wesley was particularly interested in her plan, and delighted with its results. It reminded him of what he had seen many years before in the orphan house at Halle, and among the brethren at Herrnhut. It was akin to his own endeavour at Kingswood. In his "Journal" he refers to it in the following terms: "It is exactly *Pietas Hallensis* in miniature. . . . I rode over to Leytonstone, and found one truly Christian family: that is, what that at Kingswood should be, and would, if it had such governors. . . . I preached at Leytonstone. Oh what a house of God is here! not only for decency and order, but for the life and power of religion! I am afraid there are very few such to be found in all the king's dominions."

In addition to the guidance of her household, Miss Bosanquet held services in her kitchen, at which she read and expounded the Scriptures to such of her poor neighbours as were willing to come. A Methodist class-meeting was formed, and from time to time an itinerant preacher would come and minister to the little flock.

From early morning till night there was nothing but hard
and homely toil, frugal meals, frequent religious meetings, and ever-recurring prayer and praise.   Thus de-
voting her time, her strength, her fortune to Christ and
. to the poor,

> " She filled her odorous lamp with deeds of light,
>   And hope that reaps not shame."

There was no lack of hindrances and discouragements,
however, from within and from without.   Many of the
children suffered from painful diseases, the result of
poverty and neglect.   Others distressed her with the evil
habits they had brought with them.   Her relatives spoke
of her as of one who was out of her right mind.   Some
of her critics declared that she was bringing up the
children for nuns; others said her plans savoured too
much of carnal wisdom; while others again charged her
with idleness.   Persons well-disposed and ill-disposed
poured upon her their conflicting counsels and reproofs;
and, as if the brave, lonely woman had not enough to
bear, a crowd of rough men and boys would collect at
the gate, when nights were dark, to throw dirt at the
people as they went out from the meetings, and would
afterwards come into the yard, and, putting their faces
to a window which had no 'shutters, would roar and
howl like wild beasts.

From Leytonstone Miss Bosanquet removed into
Yorkshire, and settled at Gildersome, a village near
Leeds, where she bought land and built a house.   Here
she continued for many years her self-denying labours
and let the steady light of a holy life shine, to the com-

fort and edification of many. It is not necessary to tell the story in detail; it may be enough to say that while thus living for others, her fortune was melting away, partly through injudicious generosity, and partly through the blunders of those who helped and advised her in the management of her affairs. From these causes, to which might be added the unconscionable demands of some whom she assisted, she was brought to financial embarrassment and great anxiety. At the time of Fletcher's return to England her difficulties seemed to be coming to a crisis. She saw nothing for it but to sell her Yorkshire property for what it would fetch, and with the proceeds pay off her debts as far as possible, and meet the remainder from the small income still coming to her from Leytonstone. It was at this juncture that she received an offer of marriage from Fletcher.

He was now fifty-two years of age, and Miss Bosanquet ten years younger. They had known one another for five-and-twenty years, though for the greater part of that time there was no direct intercourse between them. From their first acquaintance they had been attracted to one another. Fletcher had confessed to Charles Wesley that "Miss Bosanquet's image at one time pursued him," and that he should perhaps have lost his peace of mind if he had not betaken himself to prayer, and to a serious consideration of the reasons against matrimony. In spite of the victory thus gained, there is little doubt that her image pursued him through the following years. She, on her part, confides to her diary that a feeling "that she might be called to marry Mr. Fletcher" would now and

M

again come to her mind. She found much help and comfort in his writings. In her troubles she thought of him as "one who might perhaps be sent to her aid." She dwelt upon "some little acts of friendship in our first acquaintance," and then put the pleasant thoughts away, lest they should be a snare to her. She resolved "never to do the least thing towards a renewal of their correspondence." And so for fifteen years they never met, each of them meanwhile passing through much affliction, and needing the very help which the other could have supplied.

To Fletcher's scrupulous sense of honour, Miss Bosanquet's fortune was an effectual barrier between them. That the possession of wealth should attract unworthy suitors is nothing unusual,—it is a constantly recurring source of danger to well-dowered women ; but the danger of its repelling the worthy suitor, and so keeping those apart who are best fitted for each other, although much rarer, is perhaps even more difficult to.deal with. In such cases some sort of mediation seems desirable, though it is generally impracticable. What was wanted in this instance was, in our judgment, that some one— say Wesley, or his brother Charles—should have said to Fletcher and to Miss Bosanquet the half dozen words explanatory of each other's sentiments that would have removed all difficulty, and given them twenty years of happy married life instead of four.

It is remarkable that when Fletcher made his offer of marriage to Miss Bosanquet he had not seen her for fifteen years. There was no previous renewal of the

acquaintance, no gradual growth of intimacy and affection, no preliminaries of any kind. His proposal came
unheralded and unexpected, and was at once accepted.
It is clear that the needful preparation had been made
on both sides long ago. There was the sudden removal
of hindrances, real or imagined : that was all.

One of his letters to Miss Bosanquet, written during
their engagement, has lately been published by Mr.
Tyerman.[1] It is a true love-letter, and in no way unworthy of its writer. Others lie before us now. They
are written with the utmost freedom and simplicity, and
show a warm and tender affection, with a chivalrous
admiration for the woman soon to become his wife. The
gentle-spirited, lonely man rejoices in his new-found happiness. "Surely," he writes to her, "a human creature
alone is but *half* himself. And yet how many, for want
of having made the comparison, glory in their loss ! I
will do so no more." This is a touch of nature that the
reader will appreciate ; more particularly if he has been
at the trouble of reading the "reasons against matrimony" that have been alluded to. But we refrain from
further quotation. On the whole, we think it right to
respect the privacy of Fletcher's love-letters. They were
written for one reader, and for one only. By her they
were sacredly preserved through the thirty years of her
widowhood, and then, chiefly, we imagine, because she
could not bring herself to destroy them, they passed into
the keeping of a dear and trusted friend. To remain in

---

[1] "Wesley's Designated Successor," p. 487.

the keeping of friends, and not to be published to the
world is, in our judgment, their proper destiny.

We are, however, much indebted to Mr. Tyerman for
bringing to light the letter in which Fletcher asked the
consent of Miss Bosanquet's uncle and trustee, Mr.
Claudius Bosanquet, to his marriage with his niece.　It
is a most important piece of autobiography.　We have so
far availed ourselves of it in the course of this narrative
that the whole need not be given here.　But the following will be read with interest :

" It was soon after my ordination that I saw Miss
Mary Bosanquet, your pious niece.　I had resolved
not to marry ; but the sweetness of her temper, and
her devotedness to God, made me think that if ever
I broke through my resolution, it would be to cast
my lot with one like her.

" Not long after, at Mr. Hill's request, his nephew,
Mr. Kinaston, member for Montgomery, presented me
with the living of Madeley, a little market town in the
county of Salop, worth about £100 *per annum ;* and
here I have chiefly lived, sequestered from the world,
as your amiable niece has done at Leyton and at
Cross Hall.

" After having corresponded some years with her
on various subjects, last spring, on my return from a
journey to the continent, I ventured to mention to her
my first thoughts about a closer union with her,
thoughts which I had kept to myself for nearly twenty-
five years.　After maturely discussing the point, your
pious niece has given me room to hope she will give

me her hand, if you, sir, whom she honours as a father, give your consent to our union. I earnestly ask it, sir; and beg you will share the pleasure of uniting two persons who, from a remarkable agreement of taste, sentiments, and pursuits, as well as from a particular sympathy, seem formed for each other by the God of nature and of grace.

"I wish, sir, I had a fortune equal to Miss Bosanquet's deserts; but I hope I have one suitable to her piety, and to the moderate wishes of that godliness which, together with contentment, is a great gain. I have only about £1500 worth of property in my native country, and about £400 or £500 more in my parish, besides the income of my living, and a house much better than those with which most country clergymen are obliged to put up.

"Whatever be your pious niece's fortune, I assure you, sir, I seek her person, not her property; and to convince you of it, I request before she gives me her hand, her whole fortune may be secured to her by a proper settlement."

The same day he wrote to Miss Bosanquet's brother:

"Among the reasons which hindered me from making my addresses to your amiable sister, when first I felt that sympathy which binds my soul to hers, the superiority of her fortune was not the least. Since that time, debts, which unforeseen circumstances led her to contract, have considerably lessened that difficulty, and the prudent fear of contracting new ones seems to make it expedient for her to get into a state where she may, without difficulty and with propriety, bring her expensive housekeeping within narrower bounds. That end will at once be attained if she favours me with her hand."

The consent of Miss Bosanquet's relatives was readily and cordially given. There was indeed no such disparity in the position and circumstances of the two as could well be a ground of objection. Their Methodist friends regarded their union as a peculiarly suitable one. Wesley wrote to a friend at the time, "I should not have been willing that Miss Bosanquet should have been joined to any other person than Mr. Fletcher"; and later he said, "Miss Bosanquet was the only person in England whom I judged to have been worthy of Mr. Fletcher." They were married in Batley church, on November 12th, 1781. For nearly two months after their marriage they continued to reside at Cross Hall. It was desirable that Mrs. Fletcher's affairs should be settled before her removal to Madeley, so an arrangement was made with Mr. Crosse, the Vicar of Bradford, that he and Fletcher should exchange duty for a while. The former went to Madeley, and Fletcher took charge of Mr. Crosse's parish. On January 1st, 1782, he wrote to a friend in London: "Strangely restored to health and strength (considering my years), I have ventured to preach of late as often as I did formerly; and after having read prayers and preached twice on Christmas Day, I did last Sunday what I had never done, I continued doing duty from ten o'clock in the morning till after four in the afternoon. This was owing to christenings, churchings, and the sacrament, which I administered to a church full of people, so that I was obliged to go from the communion table to begin the evening service, and then to visit some sick. This has brought back upon me one of my old, dangerous symptoms; so I have flattered myself in vain that I should be able to do the whole duty of my own parish. My dear wife is nursing me with the tenderest care, gives me up to God with the greatest resignation, and helps me to rejoice that life and death, health and sickness, work for our good, and are all *ours*, as blessed means to forward us in our journey to heaven."

The following day Fletcher and his wife set out for Madeley.

CHAPTER XII.

LAST YEARS.

ON the first Sunday after bringing his wife to her new home, Fletcher took her into the kitchen, where, according to hospitable custom, a number of poor people were taking dinner between the morning and afternoon services, and introduced her to them, saying, "I have not married a wife for myself only, but for your sakes also." This was true, both in his intention and in the result.

In marrying Miss Bosanquet, and bringing her to Madeley, Fletcher conferred upon his parish a benefit second only to that of his own life-devotion to its welfare. During the remainder of his ministry he was sustained and supplemented in his labours by one whose qualifications were, in their sphere, little inferior to his own. She had been accustomed for many years to the direction of a large household, to the training of children and young people, to ministering to the sick and suffering. She understood the wants and ways of the poor. In these and similar respects she was exceptionally fitted to be the wife of a clergyman. The vicarage was no longer a hermitage; it was a home, a centre to which many came for help and guidance, spiritual and temporal, and from which innumerable ministries of kindness flowed out on every side. But it was in the very highest aspects of her husband's work that Mrs. Fletcher's co-operation was at once the most complete and the most valuable. Her ministry could not confine itself to the bodily and temporal welfare of the people. She too had a deep and passionate longing for the salvation of souls. To lead her poor and suffering to Christ was the one philanthropy, to which all other charities were as nothing. Toward all kinds of need her heart was full of pity, and her hand quick in bounty; but it was for the soul in each, the soul redeemed by the infinite love of God, and called to the possession of an unspeakably glorious salvation in Christ, that she was most profoundly moved. Sin was the one evil; salvation the one blessing; Christ the one Saviour. This conviction, burning with a pure, steady light and heat, ruled her work from first to last. Fletcher found in her, not only a loving wife, but a kindred spirit. They viewed personal religion under the same aspects; they were likeminded in their belief concerning the "salvation to the uttermost" that is procured by Christ, and administered by the Holy Spirit. The instinct that speaks of "the saintly Fletcher" gives the same designation to his wife. With her, as with him, Christian perfection—a term which many theological systems will not admit, and the majority of Christians persistently shun—was a chosen watchword. Their letters, journals, and devotional writings, and the lives they

were enabled to live, show that for them "death unto
sin and life unto God in Jesus Christ" was, not merely
"forensic," an "imputation," with nothing correspond-
ing to it in the sphere of experience, but included
entire consecration to God, and the unhindered in-
dwelling of the Holy Spirit. In aspiration, profession,
life, the same high utterance was repeated in different
but harmonious notes—"perfect in Christ"; always
laying more stress upon "in Christ" than upon "perfect," yet not shrinking from that term, as having
New Testament authority and significance.

For thirty years after Fletcher's death his widow
was to remain in Madeley, a presence and a power
for good; and it is this part of her life and labours
by which she is chiefly remembered. There are,
indeed, few pictures, in modern Christian history at
least, more impressive than that in which she is the
central figure, a saintly woman of great and varied
gifts, in whom Quaker-like calmness and self-control
were joined with Methodist fervour, for a whole generation a preacher of the gospel and a witness for Christ
among the people of Madeley and the neighbourhood.
The following description of her labours was written
by an eye-witness[1] of them :

"Surviving her husband many years, she lived a
'widow indeed,' doing good to all áround her, and
winning the veneration and love of rich and poor,
not only in the village and parish of Madeley, and

---

[1] Rev. W. Tranter, *Methodist Magazine*, 1837, p. 903.

in the adjoining parishes, but in all places where she was known, and to which the fame of her piety and charity had extended. The rector, not only allowed her to remain in the vicarage house undisturbed during life, but allowed her to choose the curate by whom the duties of the living were to be performed, assigning as his reason that she knew better than himself what would suit and benefit the parishioners. Besides exercising publicly, at stated times, in the vicarage room, she occasionally visited Madeley Wood, Coalbrookdale, Coalport, and other places more distant, at which times the chapels were usually crowded with delighted and profited hearers. To her house the itinerant preachers continued to come to the end of her earthly sojourn. Here they always found a hearty welcome and a delightful home. Several lovely societies were formed, others were augmented, hundreds of souls were converted, Christian believers were edified and blessed, the fruit of Mr. Fletcher's ministry was preserved, and Madeley became the *rendezvous* for religious persons and purposes—a privileged, honoured place—a sort of Christian Jerusalem. It was not uncommon to see two, three, or more clergymen, pious and able men, from neighbouring and even distant parishes, among the congregation at her week-night lectures. On the Sabbath, the pious people living at the distance of from one to four miles from Madeley usually arrived in time for her morning meeting, at nine o'clock; and, from thence, they went to the parish church, close at hand. At noon, respectable strangers, visiting Madeley for religious purposes, were usually invited to dine with her at the vicarage; the poor living too far off to allow them to return from their own houses for the after services of the day partook, if so disposed, of her hospitalities in the vicarage kitchen; others, having brought their provisions with them, were seen, in fine weather, in little companies in the fields, engaged in heavenly conversation and prayer; and others had, in an apartment to themselves, a cheap family dinner provided at the village inn.   On the ringing of a bell, at one o'clock all assembled at Mrs. Fletcher's meeting, when she was accustomed to read the life of some eminently holy man, and make remarks upon it; then they adjourned to the church for the afternoon service there and sermon; after which they repaired to their respective homes, and attended their own meeting-houses, at one or other of which the curate of Madeley officiated every Sabbath evening, as well as occasionally on the week-days, always announcing at the close of the afternoon service in the church the chapel in which he would preach that evening. This plan was adopted by Mr. Fletcher, and was followed by his evangelical and pious successors for upwards of forty years."

Returning now to the story of Fletcher's life, we feel that there was "something like prophetic strain" in the words with which he introduced his wife to his people: "I have not married a wife for myself only, but for your sakes also."

Soon after their settlement at Madeley they had a short visit from Wesley. It was near the end of March, but the rough, deep roads were blocked with snow, and it required four horses to drag his chaise from Bridgenorth. Wesley preached twice to crowded congregations, and assisted Mr. and Mrs. Fletcher to form a Christian society. Probably this part of Fletcher's work had been injured by his long absence, as we find frequent mention of such societies in the parish several years before. He lamented the decay of these means of grace, and sought Wesley's help in reviving them. This was a matter in which Wesley had unique authority and influence. In the afternoon service he therefore "enforced the necessity of Christian fellowship on all who desired either to awake or keep awake. He then desired those who were willing to join together for this purpose to call upon him and Mr. Fletcher after service. Ninety-four or ninety-five persons did so; about as many men as women. They explained to them the nature of a Christian society, and they willingly joined therein."

Three months later, Mrs. Fletcher wrote to Wesley: "The people you joined when here are, I trust, coming forward. I have not conversed with the men, but the women are more in number than at that time, . . . and on the whole there is a good increase of freedom and liberty in our class-meetings. . . .

"My dear Mr. Fletcher spares no pains; I know not which is greater, his earnest desire for souls, or his patience in bearing with their infirmities and dulness. His preaching is exceeding lively; and our sacraments are more like those in the chapels of London than any I have seen since I left it. Yet I find a great difference between the people here and those in Yorkshire."

Mrs. Fletcher accompanied her husband in his preaching excursions and visits to the religious societies within reach. She rode with him through the rain, and stood by his side, "where there was neither house nor church to cover them," while he preached to a large congregation who listened with "Yorkshire attention." It was not all smooth and easy work even now, among the ruder and more ignorant part of the people. On one occasion he writes : "I got many a hearty curse from the colliers for the plain words I spoke. . . . Had I searched the three kingdoms, I could not have found one brother willing to share gratis my weal, woe, and labours, and complaisant enough to unite his fortunes to mine; but God has found me a partner, *a sister*, *a wife*, to use St. Paul's language, who is not afraid to face with me the colliers and bargemen of my parish until death part us."

The organization of Sunday schools was, at this time, being warmly taken up by the Methodists, and by many of the clergy. Raikes established the first of his Sunday schools in Gloucester in the year 1781; but a Miss Hannah Ball, of High Wycombe, a member of the Methodist society, had established one in 1769, and probably there were also others. Though Wesley had nothing to do with originating them, he early perceived in them a great promise and possibility of good, and encouraged their formation throughout his societies. His "Journal" has this reference to them : "*July 18th,* 1784. I find these schools springing up wherever I go. Perhaps God may have a deeper end therein than men are aware of. Who knows but some of these schools may become nurseries for Christians?" At Bolton, three or four years later, he met "between nine hundred and a thousand of the children belonging to our Sunday-schools. I never saw such a sight before. They were all exactly clean, as well as plain, in their apparel. All were serious and well-behaved. Many, both boys and girls, had as beautiful faces as, I believe, England or Europe can afford. When they all sang together, and none of them out of tune, the melody was beyond that of any theatre; and what is the best of all, many of them truly fear God, and some rejoice in His salvation."

In common with Wesley, Fletcher was much impressed with the Sunday-school system as it was developing throughout the country. For some years he had maintained a day school, but he now entered vigorously upon the work of organizing Sunday schools. He issued an address to his people setting forth the evils arising from the profanation of the Lord's day, and from neglecting to educate children in the principles and practice of religion. He referred to the vices by which society was degraded and injured, and asked if nothing could be done to check these growing evils. After noticing the example set in Stroud, Gloucester, Birmingham, Manchester, and

many country parishes, he described a plan for estab-
lishing Sunday schools in the parish of Madeley. He
proposed that the children should be taught reading,
writing, and the principles of religion ; that each teacher
should be paid one shilling per Sunday ; that inspectors
should be appointed to visit the schools, to see that the
children attended regularly, and the masters did their
duty; that the schools be solemnly visited once or twice
a year, and a premium given to the children that have
made the greatest improvement. On these proposals,
subsequently modified and developed, Sunday schools
were established in Madeley, and another powerful agency
for benefiting his parishioners was brought into existence.

The labours of many years had, indeed, begun to tell,
not only on individuals, but on the general tone and
character of the community. Vice was checked and
restrained ; the people were better disposed towards
religion; the standard of morals was raised ; the conversion of notorious evil doers made its impression
upon the conscience of the careless and profane ; something like a general reformation had taken place in the
parish, and the progress of religion and morality was
now further aided by the regular religious instruction
of the young. Love for children was characteristic of
Fletcher all through life. He was never happier than
when amongst them. Before his Sunday-school was
opened, he used to meet some two or three hundred of
them on a Thursday evening, and he continued to do so
to the very week in which his last illness began. As a
result of this, a loving remembrance of him remained in

the neighbourhood where he had lived much longer than is usually the case, even with the best of men. The image of his person and character, stamped upon the hearts of children, was found sixty, seventy years afterwards, in the hearts of aged men and women.

Among the young people over whom Fletcher exercised a powerful and lasting influence was Melville Horne, who was introduced to him when seventeen years of age. At their first interview a deep impression was made upon the youth's mind, and he afterwards sought every opportunity of being in Fletcher's company. At the vicarage he came to be treated almost as a son. He subsequently received ordination, and, upon Fletcher's death, became curate of Madeley. When far advanced in life he would refer with deep feeling to his early intercourse with Fletcher. He says: "I know not which most to venerate, his public or private character. Grave and dignified in his deportment and manners, he yet excelled in all the courtesies and attentions of the accomplished gentleman. In every company he appeared as the least, the last, and the servant of all. From head to foot he was clothed with humility; while the heavenly-mindedness of an angel shone from his countenance, and sparkled in his eyes. His religion was without labour and without effort, for Christianity was, not only his great business, but his very element and nature. As a mortal man, he doubtless had his errors and failings; but what they were, they who knew him best would find it difficult to say, for he appeared as an instrument of heavenly minstrelsy, attuned to the Master's touch. . . .

N

In every view, he was a great man, and entitled to rank in the very first class of ministers ; but it was his *goodness* that raised him above all the ministers of his day."

In August, 1783; Fletcher and his wife visited Ireland. They had received a pressing invitation from the Methodists of Dublin to come over and spend a few weeks there, and help them in the good work. As long as it seemed possible to decline the invitation they had done so ; but the requests were so urgent that it seemed -to them at last that this was a call from God. Fletcher's health at the time was not good, and on various grounds they both shrank from so long and formidable a journey ; but the conviction that it was God's will settled the matter. On the day they set out they rode to Shrewsbury, paying a tribute of love and reverence to the memory of Richard Baxter as they passed through the village of Eaton Constantine, his early home. The next day they reached Llangollen, where, for want of a change of horses, they were detained for the night. A few persons who could understand English came together next morning, and Fletcher preached to them before resuming his journey.

They remained about six weeks in Dublin, and their labours were made a great blessing to many. Fletcher preached with his accustomed unction and power. His host, a gentleman of position and influence in the city, applied to the rector of the parish in which he lived to allow Mr. Fletcher to preach in his church, and this was immediately granted. The church was crowded to excess. The congregation was greatly moved ; but when

it became known that he had preached on the evening of
the same day at the Methodist chapel, all the churches
were at once closed against him, with the exception of
the Huguenot French church.   Here he preached, both
in French and in English.   Even when he preached in
French, people who could not understand a word would
be present.   "We go to look at him," they said, "for
heaven seems to beam from his countenance."   In addition to his public labours Fletcher met the members of
the society in private, and exhorted and counselled them
to their great comfort.   Mrs. Fletcher met the classes
of women.   A great revival of religion followed.   The
Methodist society increased in numbers from about five
hundred persons to upwards of a thousand, and the
spiritual life of many was deepened and enriched.

When Fletcher was about to leave them the grateful
people pressed him to accept a sum of money in pay-
ment of his expenses.   This he entirely refused to accept, until being pressed in such a manner that further
refusal seemed impossible, he consented to receive it on
condition that he might dispose of it as he pleased.   To
this they readily agreed, and every penny of it was given
to their own poor people before Fletcher and his wife
left Dublin.   A letter warmly thanking them for "your
labour of love in crossing the sea to visit us, and your
spending body and soul for our profit while among us,"
was signed by one hundred and fifty-one members of
the Dublin Methodist society, and sent after them to
Madeley.   The passage from Dublin to Holyhead was a
stormy one, but they reached their home at last in peace.

Fletcher attended one more Conference with Wesley and his preachers. It was held in Leeds in July, 1784. The great Methodist leader was now in his eighty-second year. He wrote to a friend: "When I was young I had weak eyes, trembling hands, and abundance of infirmities. But, by the blessing of God, I have out-lived them all." He laboured as hard as ever. In one respect only he spared himself; instead of riding on horseback he now made use of a travelling carriage. He still considered preaching at five o'clock in the morning the healthiest exercise in the world. He was able to preach three times a day, and address large crowds out of doors, and, when making his way to Inverness, could trudge through heavy rain twelve miles on foot. In every part of England, and very widely in Ireland and Scotland, he was better known than any other public man, and, with few exceptions, universally respected and loved. The nation had come to be proud of him. His appearance was venerable and beautiful in the extreme. The people flocked to see, as well as to hear him. He was saluted in the streets as he passed along, and chil-dren would run and kneel before him to receive his blessing.

Wesley had particular reasons for inviting Fletcher to attend the Conference. It was an anxious time with him. He had recently executed an important deed—known as the Deed of Declaration,—in which he had named one hundred of his preachers to constitute the legal Conference after his death. In this body of preachers, which had power to fill up all vacancies in its number, was vested all legal authority requisite for the admission and expulsion of preachers, the appointment of preachers to their stations; and, in various other respects, the Conference was invested with the powers hitherto possessed and exercised by Wesley himself. This deed has proved a firm foundation for the polity of the Methodists to this day. It underlies and sustains the various developments that have since taken place. It has been called Methodism's Magna Charta. Wesley himself deemed it "a foundation likely to stand as long as the sun and moon endure."

But it was not established without difficulty. There were heartburnings amongst the preachers. Of those who were not included in the "legal hundred" some were grieved, others were indignant. They could not understand on what principle Wesley had made his selection. They resented the preference shown to some, and the passing over of others among their brethren. Many of the trustees were alarmed, thinking that their powers in respect of the chapel property were imperilled. The unity of the Methodist connexion was seriously threatened, and the approaching Conference was anticipated with much anxiety. When the Conference assembled, Wesley proved himself once more equal to the occasion. His tact, his wise reasonableness, his weight of character, his transparent good faith prevailed, but it was well that he was sustained in such a crisis by the presence of Fletcher. In prospect of a heated controversy, all hope of a happy issue lay in calling forth what was deepest and best in the good men

who had come together.   Wesley knew that beneath the
irritation and resentment of the hour was a depth of
Christian principle to which appeal might hopefully be
made.

On the Sunday evening before the opening of the
Conference the congregation that assembled to hear
Wesley was so much larger than the chapel could contain, that they adjourned to a neighbouring field, where
Wesley preached a sermon on the judgment day.   Early
next morning Fletcher was the preacher, and his text
was, " Ye are the salt of the earth."   Morning and
evening, during the session of the Conference, there was
a sermon by Wesley, Fletcher, or one of the more
eminent preachers.   At the sacramental service Wesley
was assisted by Fletcher, Coke, and other clergymen.
In a sermon on " the man of God who was disobedient
to the word of the Lord," Fletcher drew such a picture
of the degradation and misery of a backsliding minister,
and of the injury he inflicted upon the Church of Christ,
as produced a deep and general sensation.   One of
his hearers reports : " I was extremely impressed with
the whole service ; the shadow of the Divine presence
was seen among us, and His going forth was in our
sanctuary."

The debate on the Deed of Declaration was the
sharpest the Conference had ever known.   Fletcher
was greatly affected.   Before the first streak of dawn his
wife heard him praying fervently for the peace and pro-
sperity of Zion, and when she gently urged him to go
to rest, he answered, " The cause of God lies near my

heart." During the discussion Fletcher "took much pains,"—to use Wesley's words. This matter-of-fact expression conveys little notion of the tender, impassioned way in which Fletcher laboured to heal the strife and prevent a schism. "Never," says a preacher who was present, "shall I forget the ardour and earnestness with which Mr. Fletcher expostulated, even on his knees, both with Mr. Wesley and the preachers. To the former he said, 'My father! my father! they have offended; but they are your children!' To the latter he exclaimed, 'My brethren! my brethren! he is your father!' And then, pourtraying the work in which they were unitedly engaged, he fell again on his knees, and with fervour and devotion engaged in prayer. The Conference was bathed in tears, many sobbed aloud."

At the close of the Conference Fletcher returned to Madeley, and resumed his quiet, pastoral life. Even yet Wesley was not quite satisfied at Fletcher's "hiding his light under a bushel" in his country parish. But the Vicar of Madeley knew his vocation, and abided by it. He wrote to his friend Mr. Ireland: "I keep in my sentry-box till Providence remove me; my situation is quite suited to my little strength. I may do as much or as little as I please, according to my weakness. And I have an advantage which I can have nowhere else in such a degree: my little field of action is just at my door; so that if I happen to overdo myself, I have but a step from my pulpit to my bed, and from my bed to my grave. . . . The snail does best in its shell; were it to aim at galloping, like the racehorse, it would be ridiculous indeed.   My wife is quite of my mind with respect to the call we have to a sedentary life."

Among the latest acquaintances made by Fletcher was that with Charles Simeon, of Cambridge, then a young and zealous clergyman just coming into note, and afterwards, for so long a period, the leader of the Evangelical party in the university.   Simeon preached in Madeley church, Fletcher himself previously going through the village, bell in hand, to announce that a young clergyman from Cambridge was about to preach, and urging the people to come to the church.

It does not appear that there was at this time any noticeable failure of strength, or appearance of dangerous symptoms ; but, in truth, his hold of life was very feeble, his vital force was almost spent.   It was often in his thoughts that death was near.   Life had never been so sweet to him as it was now ; but death too,

" Dear, beauteous death, the jewel of the just,"

was none the less the crowning mercy for which he waited.   To few men has death been so disarmed beforehand as to Fletcher.

Among the Evangelical leaders there was now, indeed, a swift succession of departures.   These "companions in tribulation, and in the kingdom and patience of Jesus Christ," were ἐπεκτεινόμενοι, "reaching forth unto" that which was before them, and one after another "attained," and was made perfect.   Early in May, 1785, Vincent Perronet, the venerable Vicar of Shoreham, died in the ninety-second year of his age.   Charles Wesley buried him, and preached his funeral sermon. He himself was, in much feebleness, awaiting his summons, and asked for Fletcher's prayers, saying, " Help me to depart in peace." He had yet three years to wait for his release.

It has been supposed that the letter, dated May 24th, 1785, in which these words occur, was the last that Fletcher received from his old and faithful friend. We are able, however, to supply a hitherto unpublished letter four weeks later in date, which is, pretty certainly, the last of the series. As will be seen, it consists in reality of three letters, one to Mrs. Fletcher, one to her and her husband conjointly, and one to Fletcher alone. They are written, however, continuously, on one sheet of paper. The fears and forebodings to which he gives expression are familiar to all who are acquainted with the history of Methodism. It will be remembered that the question of a successor to Wesley had been mentioned several years before; Charles Wesley joining with his brother in designating Fletcher to that office, and Fletcher declining it, and urging in return that, in the event of John Wesley's decease, the leadership must naturally devolve upon Charles. The latter had now made up his mind that nothing could save the Methodist societies from falling to pieces as soon as he and his brother should be removed, events that could not be far distant.

"LONDON, *June 21st,* 1785.

" MY DEAR SISTER,—

If you are weary of writing, I much more, who have

almost lost the use of my hand and eyes. You owe *me* no thanks for *my* care of you. The care of all the Churches has lain upon my brother.

"We agree in our 'willingness to be hid and forgotten.' Surely I have been *thrust out* into the harvest. If I am saved, let my memorial perish.

"When we get to the other side we shall know all ; till then our life must continue a mystery.

"Your partner was certainly given to the prayers of the people ; therefore he is their debtor so long as he lives.

"Don't you know poets are all envious ? Yet you challenge me, who never ventured at an acrostic in all my life.

"If you saw 'Sam in the cradle,' you saw him in his best estate. One out of them has some desire of salvation, but she seeks rather than strives.

"My wife and I are quite willing 'to come and see you at Madeley,' but our way is hid. It is most probable that if we ever meet again, it should be in London or Bristol. Let us help each other by our prayers at least. You will not, I know, forget your old, useless, but still affectionate servant and friend,

"C. W.

"This side is for you *both.*

"I trust you are resigned (after mine and my brother's departure) to gather up the wreck. Be sure the sheep will be scattered. All the beasts of the forest are waiting for them. Many will find shelter among the Moravians ; many will turn to the Calvinists, Baptists,

Presbyterians, and Quakers. Most, I hope, will return to the bosom of their mother, the Church of England. Not one, but several sects will arise, *and Methodism will be broken into a thousand pieces.*

"It is impossible for you to know *now*, or to divine, or to conjecture what you are intended for. Therefore the less you think about it the better, for we penetrate, we prophesy, in vain. You must stand still, and see the design and the salvation of God.

"Had I a sufficient body, I would strive to visit you, that we might compare our thoughts. So far I *can* see, that the Lord is preparing His people for some great event. But who shall live when the Lord doth this? I am far entered on my last stage, and expect every month to be my last. Providence (if you survive me) will call you to this place. My widow can tell you my mind, if worth your knowing, and show you my post-humous papers, if worth your seeing.

"Pray on, and help to a peaceful end, my beloved friends,

"Your faithful Brother,

"C. W.

"To MR. J. F.

"'Spared to keep the people,' says my dear friend? *Sed quis custodiet ipsos custodes?* The longer our time, the greater our danger of failing. I have always feared for myself that I should live a little too long. Now I fear it for my brethren also.

"Be not too sanguine for the American Methodists.

First, know their *real* condition. You justly fear that *our* Methodists should get into the prelatical spirit. I fear the fanatical spirit also. I cannot explain this in writing.

"You think I know nothing about the peace; I think you know nothing about it. Yet I wish your poem a good sale.[1]

"Happy would Sally be to die like her god-sister. I am not without hope that she will live to be a Christian. She presents her duty. We all join in love. I *need* no invitation to Madeley. While I had strength I wanted opportunity. Now I have neither."

For two or three years longer this question, 'What was to become of the Methodists after Wesley's death,' continued to exercise his brother Charles. Perhaps some anxiety would have been spared him had he acted more upon the advice he gave to Fletcher: "The less you think about it the better, for we penetrate, we prophesy, in vain. You must stand still, and see the design, the salvation of God." To this he seems finally to have come, for in one of his last letters to his brother he says: "Keep your authority while you live; and, after your death, *detur digniori*, or rather, *dignioribus*. You cannot settle the succession; you cannot divine how God will

---

[1] Fletcher had written a poem in French on the peace which, in January, 1783, had been concluded with America, France, and Spain. At the time of Charles Wesley's letter, an English version of it, by the Rev. J. Gilpin, was in the press. It appeared shortly after Fletcher's death.

settle it." Meanwhile, so far as Fletcher was concerned, he had little to learn, even from his dearest friend and counsellor, as to waiting for the Lord. No man was ever less inclined to "penetrate or prophesy." Whether he lived, he lived unto the Lord; whether he died, he died unto the Lord; living or dying, he was the Lord's. No room was left for anxiety about the future.

The summer of 1785 was an unhealthy one at Madeley. There was a good deal of fever about, "a bad, putrid fever," and Fletcher and his wife were much engaged among the sick. Two persons died within a few yards of the vicarage. Mrs. Fletcher visited them in their illness, and took the fever. "Now," she says, "I had a fresh instance of the tender care and love of my blessed partner; sickness was made pleasant by his kind attention." During this illness many thoughts passed through her mind for which she could scarcely account. Something seemed to tell her that she must yet drink deeper of the cup. She adds, "My dear husband and I are led to offer ourselves to do and suffer all the will of God." The time was fast approaching when this submission to the will of God was to have its crowning test.

On Thursday, August 4th, Fletcher was busy amongst his flock from three in the afternoon till nine at night. On returning home he said, "I have taken cold." During the two following days he went about much as usual, though with some difficulty. On Saturday night he was very feverish, and his wife begged him not to go to church in the morning, but to let one of the Methodist preachers who was staying with them preach in the churchyard ; but he replied that it was the will of the Lord that he should go.   The morning came, and he began the service at the usual hour.   While reading the prayers he almost fainted.   His wife pressed through the crowd, and entreated him to leave the reading-desk and come home.   In his gentle manner he bade her let him go on.   The windows were opened, and he seemed a little refreshed as he proceeded with the service.   When prayers were ended he ascended the pulpit, and gave out his text, "How excellent is Thy lovingkindness, O God ! therefore the children of men put their trust under the shadow of Thy wings."   After the sermon he went up the aisle to the communion table, saying, " I am going to throw myself under the wings of the cherubim, before the mercy-seat."   The congregation was large, and the service lasted till nearly two o'clock.   He was often obliged to stop for want of power to speak.   The people were deeply affected ; nearly all were in tears.

As soon as the service was over he was hurried away to bed, and immediately fainted.   During the three following days he was restless in body, but in mind alternately calm, and filled with holy joy.   Again and again he would say, "God is love, God is love." His symptoms were still thought to be not unfavourable. On Thursday, the 11th, his speech began to fail, but when he could say nothing else to be understood, he would repeat " God is love."   The next day his faithful wife felt a sword pierce through her soul as she found his body covered with spots. She knelt by his bed, with her hand in his, and entreated the Lord to be with them both. On the afternoon of Saturday he stretched out his hand to each of the friends who stood around him. His wife said to him : " My dear, I ask not for myself, but for the sake of others; if Jesus is very present with thee, lift thy right hand." He did so. She added, " If the prospect of glory opens before thee, repeat the sign." He raised his hand again ; and, in half a minute, a second time.

The end was fast drawing near. It was Sunday evening, and the church was filled with a weeping con- gregation offering up their prayers for their dying pastor. At the conclusion of the service the people lingered about the vicarage, and seemed unable to go to their homes. Many of them were admitted to the house, and allowed to pass by the open door of his room, where they could see him, propped up with pillows in his bed. His countenance continued unaltered, but his weakness perceptibly increased. He sank into a kind of sleep, and at half-past ten o'clock on Sunday night, August 14th, 1785, Fletcher of Madeley breathed his last, in the fifty-sixth year of his age.

Three days afterwards he was buried in Madeley churchyard amid the tears and lamentations of his people.

The inscription on his tombstone was written by his widow. A longer and more detailed epitaph, from the pen of Richard Watson, in City Road Chapel, sets forth his character and labours. Fletcher of Madeley will continue to be remembered for what he did, but still more for what he was. "The righteous shall be in everlasting remembrance."

APPENDIX.

EXTRACTS from Fletcher's manuscript "Book of Devotions," referred to on p. 38.

CHRISTIANA PRÆCEPTA.

Contemplare Dei Natum, legesque benignas ;
Omnia te Christi vita docere potest.

Appage te mea mens absisque philautia longè,
Filius ipse Dei sua nunquam vota secutus.
Ut mea vota Deo mactarem, se duce, lætus
Sponte sua summo paruit patri inter olivas.

Porcina qui quærit Divina solamina perdit.
Ne dapium ventrisque tui mala gaudia quæras ;
Mens tibi pura nequit saturato ventre vigere.
Cibus enim nimius Divinæ particulam auræ
Certo affigit humi Cœlique afflamine privat.

Ne doleas si pauper habes seu scommata mundi,
Seu risus hominum titulos et prædia sola ;
Pauper cum Christus vilique a plebe jocatus
In turpi ligno vitam componat amaram.

RESISTE TENTATIONI HIS CONSILIIS.

Dæmona ne dubita te certo vincere posse,
Hunc tunc haud dubio Christo auxiliante fugabis.

Ne ruas in vetitum, brevis est et fluxa Libido :
Sperne Voluptatem, dirum ponè linquit acumen.
Crede mihi, Satanæ minimam ne cedito partem ;
Fortiter ac subito plagam repelle priorem.
Numinis auxilium precibus rogato benignis.
In cruce pro culpis morientem cernito Jesum.
Cœlestes palmas, et Tartara dira memento.
Offert judicium cita mors, hilaremque triumphum.
Viribus indomitis, rigidisque resistito membris
Dæmonis impetibus ; Christus hunc *appage* vicit.
Vivida sit fides, te certa corona manebit.

There is no need either to point out, or to apologize
or, the shortcomings of Fletcher's Latin verses.   They
are little more than private memoranda for use in prayer
and meditation, written in Latin, perhaps, as a kind of
cipher.   The following resolutions are interesting :

" Hæc Deo juvante facere decerno.
    3 edere die. quod ubi primum violaverim, pauperibus
b. asses dandi et venia per horam petenda erit, nullo fulcro
utens.
    Pueros nunquam ob doctrinam castigare, sub eâdem pœnâ.
    Precans nunquam jacere, sed stare vel genu flectere."

This may be translated :

These things, God helping me, I determine :
To take food three times a day ; for a breach of this rule,
twopence to be given to the poor, and pardon to be implored
for an hour, using no bodily support.
    Never to punish the boys for their lessons, under the same
penalty.
    Never to lie down while engaged in prayer, but stand or
kneel.

Le Bonheur du Chrétien.

Heureux qui n'a point de désir,
Heureux qui se fait violence,
Qui se prive des vains plaisirs,
Et se plaît dans la dépendance.
Heureux l'homme de bonne foi,
Simple, sage, plein d'innocence,
Qui, toujours sévère pour soi,
Pour son prochain est rempli de clémence.

Heureux qui chérit le silence,
Qui ne parle que utilement,
Et se repose uniquement
Sur la Divine Providence.

Heureux qui connaissant son extrême indigence
L'expose au ciel incessamment,
Et qui de son Dieu seulement
Attend toute son assistance.
Heureux qui n'a rien d'affecté,
Heureux l'homme sans volonté,
Et qui, vide de lui même,
Est tout plein du vrai Dieu qu'il aime.

Heureux qui pénétré des besoins du prochain
Lui partage son cœur, son Esprit, et son pain.
Heureux celui qui l'édifie.
Heureux celui qu'on humilie,
Et qui sait profiter de ses abaissements.
Heureux qui n'a jamais de vertus chimériques,
Et qui chérit ses domestiques
Comme s'ils étaient ses enfants.
Heureux qui ne va point par des routes obliques,
Heureux, plus heureux qu'on ne croit,
Qui marche constamment dans le chemin étroit.
Heureux qui par ses soins, par son économie,
Sait amasser pour l'autre vie,

Et ménager si bien ses précieux moments
Qu'il n'en pert pas un seul en vains amusements.
Heureux qui se voit sans attache,
Qui se fait petit, qui se cache,
Et qui ne suit jamais ses propres mouvements.
Heureux qui sur la grace uniquement se fonde,
Qui sait, et ne croit rien savoir.
Qui peut, et qui n'a du pouvoir,
Que pour obliger tout le monde.
Heureux celui qui du Sauveur
S'Efforce d'être la copie.
Heureux celui de qui le cœur
Goute la parole de vie.
Heureux qui sait aimer, craindre, croire, espérer,
Comme le fait un vrai fidèle.
Heureux qui sait persévérer,
Et soumettre a l'esprit une chair si rebelle.
Heureux l'homme nouveau, qui souvent dans son cœur
Trouve une utile, douce, et sainte solitude,
Et qui fait toute son étude
De la croix de son Rédempteur.
Heureux le grand sans tyrannie ;
Heureux le petit sans envie ;
Heureux l'homme toujours égal,
Qui ne pense d'autrui ni ne dit aucun mal.
Heureux qui gémit et qui prie
Pour le prochain comme pour soi,
Et qui sent pour le vice une horreur infinie.
Heureux qui se fait une loi
De son devoir qu'il aime, et qu'il veut toujours suivre.
Heureux qui souffre tout et ne fait rien souffrir ;
Heureux celui qui sait bien vivre,
C'est le moyen de bien mourir.

Butler & Tanner, The Selwood Printing Works, Frome, and London.

www.ingramcontent.com/pod-product-compliance
Lightning Source LLC
Chambersburg PA
CBHW030829020726
47499CB00006B/2131